THE PHENOMENAL SUCCESS STRATEGIES OF DR. ROBERT ANTHONY HAVE MOTIVATED MILLIONS TO REACH FOR SUCCESS —AND TAKE IT!

When *desire* meets *opportunity*, exciting things begin to happen! If you have never been able to accept this, or even to recognize opportunity for what it is, it is undoubtedly because you have been concentrating on something else. Perhaps you have allowed yourself to become preoccupied with a lot of negative input—all the "reasons" why something *may not work*.

Negative thoughts generate fear, anxiety and discouragement. Once you allow these negative thoughts to become dominant *beliefs*, they are certain to undermine your plans, and failure is the inevitable result. You literally end up sabotaging your ability to become a Winner.

Desire, on the other hand, is a creative force. It helps you to accept what you want to accomplish and it inspires enthusiasm. The sum is your *belief* in your ability to succeed. Remember, "*As a man thinketh, in his heart, so is he.*"

Berkley Books by Dr. Robert Anthony

HOW TO MAKE A FORTUNE FROM PUBLIC SPEAKING:
PUT YOUR MONEY WHERE YOUR MOUTH IS

THINK

THINK AGAIN

THE ULTIMATE SECRETS OF TOTAL SELF-CONFIDENCE

DR. ROBERT ANTHONY'S ADVANCED FORMULA FOR
TOTAL SUCCESS

DR. ROBERT ANTHONY'S MAGIC POWER OF SUPER
PERSUASION

50 IDEAS THAT CAN CHANGE YOUR LIFE

DOING WHAT YOU LOVE, LOVING WHAT YOU DO

BETTING ON YOURSELF

BETTING ON YOURSELF

STEP-BY-STEP STRATEGIES for The TOTAL WINNER

Dr. Robert Anthony

BERKLEY BOOKS, NEW YORK

BETTING ON YOURSELF

A Berkley Book / published by arrangement with
ROI Associates, Inc.

PRINTING HISTORY
Berkley trade paperback edition / November 1991

ISBN: 0-425-13038-X

A BERKLEY BOOK® TM 757,375
Berkley Books are published by The Berkley Publishing Group,
200 Madison Avenue, New York, New York 10016.
The name "BERKLEY" and the "B" logo
are trademarks belonging to Berkley Publishing Corporation.

PRINTED IN THE UNITED STATES OF AMERICA

10 9 8 7 6 5 4 3 2

Contents

AUTHOR'S NOTE.................................... vii

1 BETTING ON YOURSELF—PUTTING THE
ODDS IN YOUR FAVOR............................ 1

2 LUCK—HOW IT INFLUENCES OUR LIVES 12

3 PROBABILITY VS. SUPERSTITION............ 22

4 THE EBB AND FLOW OF CHANCE............ 32

5 HOW OTHERS INFLUENCE YOUR WIN
FACTOR... 43

6 INTUITIVE FEELINGS—HOW TO TAKE
ADVANTAGE OF THEM 54

7 HOW WINNERS THINK RICH AND
GET RICH... 68

8 HOW THE "ATTITUDE OF GRATITUDE"
INCREASES YOUR WIN FACTOR.............. 83

9 "WIN THERAPY"—A MODEL OF SUCCESS 96

10 CREATING A WINNING LIFE-SCRIPT........ 105

11 MAKING A GOOD LUCK WHEEL OF
FORTUNE TO OBTAIN YOUR DESIRES 119

12 WHAT TO DO WHEN YOUR SHIP
COMES IN 129

13 TEN ATTRIBUTES ALL WINNERS HAVE
IN COMMON... 140

Author's Note

Several years ago I became interested in handicapping thoroughbred race horses as a hobby. In case you are not familiar with the term "handicapping" as applied to race horses, it simply means *eliminating the horses in a race you feel will lose and selecting the one horse you feel will win*. That's the first step.

The next step concerns itself with betting on the winner. Before any handicapper bets on a winner, he must be sure in his own mind that he has chosen a winner and not a loser. The amount of money he bets generally depends upon the odds the horse is paying.

There is nothing particularly unusual in my interest in all this except that I had spent most of my life using my talents and abilities as a psychotherapist and personal development trainer. Handicapping horses was far removed from anything I had ever been trained to do. Or was it?

Our lives come together in mysterious ways. We continually set ourselves up to learn new lessons and to increase our awareness. In this case, it suddenly came to me that the process of betting on a winner at the racetrack was exactly the same as betting on oneself to win at whatever one chose to accomplish. In other words, we have to eliminate our losing patterns and choose winning patterns that will assist us in accomplishing our goals and objectives.

This book is not about gambling or picking winners at the racetrack, although I think you will find the parallel examples to be interesting and very useful in helping you to have more of what *you* want. This book will expose you to new ideas and concepts that will enable you to win at almost anything you do. You will discover that the patterns for winning are the same for any endeavor.

After learning what is required, you will be asked to place a "bet" on yourself. Betting on yourself is the risk you must take to see if your beliefs about winning and losing are correct.

The advantage you have is that I have personally experienced everything discussed in this book and, to the best of my ability, have refined a system that can be used to dramatically increase your odds of winning.

Bear in mind that these are MY ideas, not yours. They can only BECOME yours once you have proven them to be true for you. The only way this can possibly be done is through daily application.

It all boils down to this: *The best bet you can ever make in life is on YOURSELF!* Believe in yourself and believe in your right to have what you want, and you will be a Winner!

Now then, let's start at the beginning...

CHAPTER 1
Betting On Yourself— Putting The Odds In Your Favor

This book is concerned with winning. More specifically, it is concerned with winning the most important game of all—the Game of Life! If you are determined to create a rewarding job or career opportunity, to succeed in your relationships, to become financially secure, and to enjoy a sense of emotional and spiritual well-being, this book can assist you in becoming a Winner in all these areas.

The path to winning is reasonably straight. There are, however, a number of obstacles that need to be overcome along the way. For some, these obstacles may seem insignificant. For others, they may appear to be insurmountable. Whatever your own feelings might be, you can be sure they have been greatly influenced by your childhood programming—whatever your parents, friends, teachers, religious leaders and peer groups have programmed you to believe about yourself. Their influence has profoundly affected your odds of winning at any endeavor you choose to undertake.

WINNING IS AN ATTITUDE

To understand what it takes to beat the odds against losing, you must first understand what it takes to be a Winner. Contrary to popular belief, winning is NOT a matter of luck. Winning is an attitude.

For the purpose of this study, we will divide the general population into three specific categories:

1. Winners
2. Losers
3. Non-Winners

WINNER—This is a person who has what he wants. He is someone who is accustomed to achieving his goals. In the end, he achieves whatever he sets out to accomplish.

LOSER—This is a person who doesn't have what he wants, but has good "reasons" why he doesn't have it. He feels he is a "victim" of people, circumstances and conditions. If asked, he will generally admit he feels "trapped" or "stuck".

NON-WINNER—This is a person who is willing to do whatever it takes to be a Winner, but who lacks the necessary knowledge and skills to go from where he is to where he wants to be. A Non-Winner realizes that whatever is happening in his life is a situation of his own making. He does not blame family, friends, some historical event in his life, his environment or God for his present situation. Nor does he blame himself. He realizes that through greater knowledge and desire, he can make some significant changes. Recognizing his present situation as a *temporary* one, he is willing to do whatever is necessary to get on the path that leads to winning.

If you are not presently a Winner, you are either a Loser or a Non-Winner. As a Loser, you cannot have what you want until you are willing to take the first step. This requires giving up all excuses or "reasons" for not having what you want. It also means no longer identifying with or attempting to justify your "victim" status. Once a Loser is able to do this, he will automatically move up into the Non-Winner category. As a Non-Winner, it now becomes possible to practice and eventually master the necessary skills to become a Winner.

THE STARTING POINT TO BECOMING A WINNER

The initial starting point on the path to winning is the willingness to pay the price for what you want. What separates Losers from Winners is the Loser's compulsive need for immediate gratification. Losers are reluctant to invest their time, effort and money in *advance* unless they can be assured of an immediate return. Winners, on the other hand, are willing to pay the price in *advance*, knowing they can only receive in direct proportion to what they are willing to expend.

THE FIRE OF DESIRE

The willingness to expend time, money and energy to have what you want requires a strong *desire*. The more you desire to go from being a Loser or Non-Winner to a Winner, the less likely you will accept anything else.

When *desire* meets *opportunity*, exciting things begin to happen! If you have never been able to accept this, or even to recognize opportunity for what it is, it is undoubtedly because you have been concentrating on something else. Perhaps you have allowed yourself to become preoccupied with a lot of negative input—all the "reasons" why something *may not work*. That too takes thought and energy, and in the end, it may take all you have.

Negative thoughts generate fear, anxiety and discouragement. Once you allow these negative thoughts to become dominant *beliefs*, they are certain to undermine your plans, and failure is the inevitable result. You literally end up sabotaging your ability to become a Winner.

Desire, on the other hand, is a creative force. It helps you to accept what you want to accomplish and it inspires enthusiasm. The sum is your *belief* in your ability to succeed. Remember, "*As a man thinketh, in his heart, so is he.*"

THE VIEW DEPENDS
ON THE POINT OF VIEW

Beating the odds means making the necessary changes to turn those odds *in your favor*. Whether you realize it or not, success, or the lack of it, is *absolutely predictable*. We always have two choices. One is to accept success as the natural order of things. The other is to accept failure in the same way.

If we do not choose to activate our inner success mechanism, our failure mechanism will *automatically* become engaged since it is *already programmed in us through past conditioning*. To adopt a winning attitude is to make sure that your failure mechanism doesn't take control of your life experiences.

OPPORTUNITIES OR OBSTACLES?

By nature, we are not victims but creators, and all creation begins with belief. In this case, if you believe something will work, you will see *opportunities*. If you believe something will not work, you will see *obstacles*. The problem with seeing only obstacles is that you tend to add other obstacles to them. By way of example:

I recently met with a man who was concerned about his overall health. His rather sedentary life had caused him to gain some undesired weight, and because he had been feeling unusually lethargic and depressed, he had gone to see his doctor.

"My doctor tells me I need to adopt a physical fitness program," he said, almost as if a death sentence had been pronounced for him. "The thing is, I really hate to exercise! Even so, I went out and priced some good exercise equipment, which created *another* problem. The good stuff is pretty expensive. Lately, I've been thinking about taking up some form of passive exercise, you know, something like walking—but the thing is, I'm always pressed for time. Then too, it's really hard to get into that kind of thing if you're not athletically inclined. The way I figure it, there isn't much point in trying to be something you're not. Oh well, nobody lives forever!"

I was extremely amused, and very nearly laughed aloud at how quickly this person was able to talk himself OUT of the need to exercise and INTO an early grave. Although this type of reasoning was certainly not new to me, quite frankly, I had never seen it accomplished with such incredible speed!

We concluded our conversation that day by discussing the manner in which a negative can sometimes turn into a positive. I suggested that this man look beyond his own immediate dislike for exercise, and that he try to find something beneficial (an opportunity) in what he perceived to be an unobtainable objective (an obstacle).

I did not really expect to hear from him again, but one day I did. He sounded excited and enthusiastic on the phone. We met for lunch and I noticed at once he was slimmer and trimmer, and that he seemed extremely energetic and alive! "I did what you suggested," he said, causing me to wonder what part I had actually played in all of this. Before I could even ask, he told me the rest of the story.

"It occurred to me that there are any number of people who hate to exercise, just as I do. I figured there must be other types of exercise that would be beneficial but not as strenuous as aerobic classes, weight lifting or running. So, I went to the library and checked out everything I could find on the subject. With the information I gathered, I put together a special physical fitness class based on nonstrenuous isometric exercises. They are easy to do and build up strength and endurance. They are an excellent way to shape or contour the body.

"I then ran an ad in the paper that was specifically worded to attract people who felt they needed an exercise program but were the nonphysical types. I received dozens of calls. The first night of the class, a total of twenty-one people showed up. I'm charging them thirty-five dollars for a ten-week class. Can you believe it? Now I'm actually being paid to keep myself in shape and to help others do the same!"

As I listened to this story, I thought again how quickly, how easily an obstacle can be turned into an opportunity. Do you see any way of applying this man's experiences to your own life? Are there some obstacles in your life that can be turned into opportunities? If so, why not start now by viewing your obstacles as hidden opportunities for success?

LEARN FROM OTHER WINNERS

As you make the transition from a Loser to a Non-Winner to a Winner, you will invariably receive advice from others on what you "should" do and the probability of your success if you are smart enough to heed their advice. With all this advice available, and most of it free, it is important to examine the *source* and *validity* of the advice to determine if it is true or false. Ask yourself: "Is the person who is giving me this advice a Winner?" This is especially important if you are presently living a Loser lifescript.

Unfortunately, Losers don't listen to Winners. They tend to take their advice from other Losers. They frequently take their financial advice from well-meaning family and friends who can't pay their bills. They discuss marital problems with those who rarely, if ever, manage to make a success out of their relationships. They discuss their plans, dreams and goals with those who have never achieved much, and whose fears will naturally cause them to discourage any idea that involves risk, imagination or delayed gratification.

One of the *games* Losers play is to make sure other potential Winners stay stuck where they are. Losers are not in the habit of letting other Losers win. If they allowed them to win, it would force them to realize that their opinions and ideas are invalid. Losers would rather be "right" about their reason for losing, than to be "wrong" about their ideas for not winning. That's why they stay Losers.

The best advice I can give you is to start listening to Winners. And the first thing a Winner is apt to caution you about is the negativity of others.

"Don't expect to be understood," a Winner may well be inclined to say. "No one can possibly feel what you are feeling, or want what you want, or achieve something in quite the same way that you can. Expect others to be blind to your vision since they can't really identify with it. But that doesn't make it wrong."

When you first start out on the path to winning, it is important to understand that what is wrong for someone else is not necessarily wrong for you. As long as you are honest and sincere in your desires, and also *well-intentioned*, you have every right to pursue your dream, and should never let the advice of a Loser convince you that you are wrong for wanting what you want.

LIGHTS! CAMERA! NOW WHAT?

In the film industry, the call is generally for "Lights! Camera! Action!" In your own life, it is much the same. Once the light of some new idea has focused itself firmly in your mind, your mind's eye (the camera) begins to visualize what you are actually trying to achieve. After that, it's time to take action! But nothing will happen unless you are *motivated* to take action.

A Loser must be motivated to change into a Non-Winner. A Non-Winner must be motivated to change into a Winner. Unfortunately, most people are "Deficiency Motivated," which simply means that they believe that there is actually something *wrong* with them, that they are *deficient* in some way. The truth is that there is nothing *deficient* or *wrong* with you. The deficiency is in your belief about yourself. The problem is not with WHO YOU ARE but rather with WHAT YOU HAVE ACCEPTED FOR YOURSELF. The reason you may feel deficient or inadequate to change your Loser life-script to that of a Winner is that you may have accepted the idea that what you want is not really possible for you.

YES YOU CAN!

The starting point of any change is the belief that it is possible to change. Yet, so many people find it difficult to make positive changes. The reason for this is that we have been programmed or "convinced" that we are powerless. Powerlessness comes from a "No I can't" deficiency belief system.

It has been estimated that by the age of eighteen, the average person has heard the word "NO!" over 150,000 times! That is enough to establish a Loser pattern. Researchers have also estimated that approximately 75 percent of everything we think about is thought of in a negative self-defeating or counterproductive way. Year after year we continue to be inundated with negative messages that gradually become part of our life-script. Not surprisingly, we begin doing it to ourselves. On a daily basis, we begin chipping away at our confidence and self-esteem in a truly demoralizing way.

If you are going to put the odds in your favor and turn your life into a winning pattern, you must stop allowing any "You can't" or "I can't" thoughts to dominate your consciousness. Simply put—"If you think you can—you CAN! If you think you can't—you CAN'T! Either way, you will be right!"

THE PROBLEM IS NOT THE PROBLEM

You may think your life is so full of problems that you will never solve them all. And you're right! But the problem is not the problem. Not only is there nothing wrong with you, but there is nothing wrong with having problems.

A problem is simply the difference between where you are and where you want to be. Problems are what fill in the space between the starting point and the end result, or goal. You are always going to have problems because once you solve one, another will fill in that space! That isn't good or bad. It simply IS!

The only people who don't have problems are those who are buried in cemeteries. Problems signify our need for change. Sometimes the world seems crazy because there are so many problems. But it has been that way since the beginning of time. Every generation thought their problems were worse than those of the generation before them. The truth is, no one's problems are worse than anyone else's. They're just *different!*

CHANGE IS THE ORDER OF THE UNIVERSE

Everything in the universe, including you, is constantly undergoing change. Since change is inevitable, it should be welcomed instead of feared. People are baffled, confused, even panicked by the idea of change. Their major aim in life is to see how few changes they can make while holding onto what they have. As if such a thing were even possible! Whatever the present course of your life, I promise you that it is already undergoing change. Some of it is obvious and some of it is gradual, subtle in a way you can barely perceive.

Another interesting thing about change—particularly as it relates to our lives—is that it always seems to imply something *bad*. A change in personal relationships, or in one's employment or financial situation, is generally anticipated in a negative light. As if such circumstances or conditions could only get *worse*—never better! Why do you think this assumption is made? Again, it goes back to our *belief* about change. Something only you can *change*. Ah yes, there is that ugly word again! But in this case, change is a positive word, one that will assist you in becoming a Winner at almost everything you do.

WHO IS RESPONSIBLE?

Who is responsible for *what*? Your happiness? Your success? Your health? Your finances? Who do you think?

Although it may be more comforting to believe that your parents, your boss, your mate, your environment, or society in general is responsible for what you have or don't have, the truth is that you created everything in your life through your choices. Your choices make you the person you are. You consciously and unconsciously make choices that determine whether you will be a Loser, a Non-Winner or Winner. Whatever you have inside of you is not the result of what somebody put there. IT IS THE RESULT OF WHAT YOU DECIDE TO KEEP INSIDE OF YOU!

Let's use an orange as an example. If you squeeze an orange, what do you get? You get what's inside. It doesn't take a mental giant to figure out that you will get orange juice. Why? Because THAT'S WHAT IS INSIDE!

Using the same analogy, if you squeeze a person, what do you get? YOU GET WHAT'S INSIDE. If there is a Loser pattern inside, then the outside life pattern will be that of a Loser. So, it isn't the *who, what* or *how* that causes you to be the way you are. It is your *acceptance* of the belief that causes you to behave the way you do. Keep in mind that if you don't hold something inside of you, it can never come out! If you don't keep negative beliefs inside of you, they can never affect your life. Again, you have to make the choice.

Start now by realizing that everything that is happening to you in life at this moment—you have a voice in! You can change anything you want if you are motivated enough. The motivation must be to let go of any Loser patterns and substitute them with Winner patterns. This is done by changing your life-script, which we will discuss in detail in later chapters. For now, you must begin by accepting that change is not only *necessary* but *entirely possible*. And who is responsible for that change? You guessed it. It's YOU!

OUT WITH THE OLD— IN WITH THE NEW

Responsibility and Change. Two words that often cause fear in the hearts of those who should actually be delighted that such an option exists. Contrary to popular opinion, responsibility does not imply a *duty* or *burden*. It is actually our willingness to accept life and to fulfill ourselves according to our individual talents and desires. Responsibility is also closely linked to our determination to succeed. OUR determination, not someone else's.

When you were a child, you may have expressed a desire to become a teacher, writer, police officer, nurse, or entrepreneur. Can you remember your parents' reactions to what you had expressed? Were they supportive or were they *determined* to change your mind? In the end, someone's determination won out. Perhaps it was yours. Perhaps it was theirs. If you ended up becoming a doctor because so many other members of your family had chosen that profession, it is highly possible that you are not happy today. In fact, you would fit our description of a Loser, even if you are a very *good* doctor.

While others may look up to you, you will always feel like a Loser because you did not assume responsibility for becoming what you really wanted to be. The sad fact is that a great majority of people fall into this category and, in later years, tend to speak fondly of an earlier "lost" dream.

"It was always an impractical idea," they will say in their own defense. "I mean—my chances of actually becoming a (fill in the blank) were not realistic. Still, I've often wondered how things might have worked out if I had pursued such a career. Oh well, I guess I'll never know."

Do you know anyone like this? Is it you? Are you beginning to see that we are responsible for the choices we make? If so, I urge you to accept the idea that IT IS NEVER TOO LATE TO CHANGE.

Changing your life-script from that of a Loser to that of a Non-Winner to that of a Winner is something that you can do with the proper knowledge and determination. It won't be difficult unless you CHOOSE to make it difficult. I'll remind you again—everything is a choice.

The best investment you can make is to BET ON YOURSELF. You can be sure that by betting on yourself, you can put the odds of success in your favor.

It is not a matter of *luck* but a matter of taking advantage of *chance opportunities* that are constantly available if we know how to recognize them.

CHAPTER 2
Luck—How It Influences Our Lives

Are you a gambler? How often do you gamble? Do you consider yourself "lucky" or "unlucky"? Overall, is your gambling confined to the racetrack, to sports betting, casinos, or do you participate in other forms of gambling as well? Perhaps you are an individual who believes that all forms of gambling are wrong, and that it is best to abstain entirely.

As an abstainer, have you ever found yourself saying: "I'll bet that (this or that) is going to happen?" The fact is, we are ALL gamblers. We gamble every time we cross the street that we are going to reach the other side. We gamble when we get into our car that we won't have an accident. We gamble when we start a new business that it will succeed. When we marry, we are gambling that the marriage will work out. In short, any situation that involves financial, physical or emotional risk is a gamble.

The decision to assume risk is generally determined by what we perceive the odds to be. If we feel the odds are in our favor, we are most apt to take action—otherwise, we will generally wait until we feel the odds have improved to a point where the benefits now outweigh the risks.

Being "lucky" is directly related to the odds, or the chances of a specific event taking place. Attracting good luck and good fortune is simply a matter of placing the odds in your favor.

I have spent many years learning to handicap thoroughbred racehorses. It has proven to be both a pleasurable and profitable hobby. Through my own ability to lessen the odds of losing, and by *increasing* the odds of winning, I have managed to become a consistent winner at the track.

While many losers may blame "bad luck" or claim that the race is fixed, in actuality, they have not yet learned how to properly apply the laws of probability. NOTE: A wager should only be made when the R.O.I. (Return on Investment) is in your favor. Professional handicappers know this and pass up all other wagers, preferring to rely upon proven percentages.

CREATING THE LUCK YOU DESIRE

Since luck is so unpredictable, it has become a conditioned response to assume that it is beyond our control. For those who have come to accept this, bad luck is often an excuse or face-saving device that is used to justify failure.

Make no mistake about it! With very few exceptions, we create the events and experiences in our lives that cause us to be lucky or unlucky. Barring certain unpredictable and catastrophic occurrences such as earthquakes, floods, hurricanes, or incurable diseases, I can assure you that you have the ability to create good luck in your life with mathematical certainty. It is simply a matter of turning "chance" into "good luck" through the right mental, emotional, spiritual and physical environment in order for good luck and good fortune to be manifested.

If you will read this chapter in a careful and conscientious way, I am certain your ideas about luck will begin to change. It will become altogether clear to you that luck has nothing to do with outside forces. You will begin to understand that being "lucky" is determined by a specific condition of mind which enables you to create the circumstances you desire.

The fact that we can create good or bad luck through our thoughts and actions is a concept that many people refuse to consider. Why? Because it immediately makes them responsible for what is happening and for what *may* happen in the future. This can be extremely disturbing to those who prefer to believe that they are simply "plagued" with bad luck, notwithstanding the fact that they are honest, hard-working, extremely likable and well-intentioned. Such people often insist that life has simply dealt them the "wrong cards" and that there is nothing they can do about it.

To say there is nothing you can do about your immediate circumstances is to say that you lack the personal capabilities or potential to make any positive changes in your life. Do you believe this is true? I very much doubt it. It only stands to reason that the years have taught you through education and experience. And what of the personal aptitudes and talents that have brought you this far? If you possessed them in the past, you may be sure that you still possess them today.

NATURAL ABILITY VS. POTENTIAL

Most self-help books or cassette tapes invariably get around to discussing the subject of "potential." The author or narrator will usually attempt to motivate the listener or reader on the basis of the theory that we, as human beings, are gifted with "unlimited potential." We are repeatedly told that the key to unlocking this potential is in our minds, and that whatever we can conceive we can also achieve.

To avoid any confusion or misunderstanding in the matter, let me say at the outset that I am in total agreement with the concept of untapped, unlimited potential. But while this may be true in the abstract, it becomes somewhat unrealistic through practical application.

Our own failure and disappointment are often perpetrated by our inner confusion between potential and natural ability.

By way of example: While I certainly have the *potential* to become a musician, I do NOT have the natural ability. Some years ago, I learned this the hard way. After spending hundreds of hours attempting to learn to play a musical instrument, I found I was no better at it than the first day I started taking lessons. The unhappy truth of the matter was, while I possessed the potential and also the motivation to play an instrument, I possessed no natural ability.

At the risk of sounding esoteric, I feel it is important for me to share some background thought on the subject of natural ability. As a direct result of my reading, study, research and personal experience, I believe that each of us comes into this world already equipped with natural abilities that will insure our success and happiness if these are properly recognized, nurtured and developed. A case in the extreme is that of the child prodigy. Many such children have been known to play a musical instrument, or to even *compose* music without any encouragement or formal instruction. How are such things possible?

Again, based on my own experience in working with such gifted individuals, I am inclined to believe that these people were born with these highly developed natural abilities. Perhaps they "learned" them in another lifetime. There is no way of telling. But to merely chalk it up to coincidence or some random genetic aberration is not reasonable or acceptable to me.

The point I am trying to make here is that we have the potential to do *many* things, the natural ability to do a *few*, and possibly only *one* with any real quality of excellence.

Remember! Good luck and good fortune are highly dependent upon a realistic understanding of your personal abilities and limitations. When viewed in the proper context, the combination of desire and true ability can prove to be a powerful force indeed!

GETTING A CLEAR PICTURE

In order to most effectively take advantage of "chance" opportunities, it is first necessary to distinguish between random opportunities and opportunities that are in alignment with our own natural talents and abilities. If we have a totally realistic view of what we are capable of accomplishing, we will not be tempted to enter into situations that must inevitably be doomed to failure.

Moral of the Story: Make the most of who you are—who you REALLY are, and never try to be something you are not. Seek to live within your true mental, physical, psychological, economic and spiritual capacity, and you will never cultivate the unfortunate circumstances that others typically refer to as "bad luck."

Although you may be told that you can do anything if you try, the fact is, you may not really want to. By functioning beyond the parameters of your own personal talents and abilities, you will soon reach a point of diminishing return, and thereafter, suffer needless stress, frustration and concern.

While this is certainly a situation to be avoided, it is equally wrong to *underestimate* your capabilities, or to hold yourself back because of an irrational need to "play it safe." I have known many people who have successfully completed the first phase of their careers, which is to say that they are now ready to move a bit further up the ladder. But while they have the skills, the experience and every other necessary qualification, they refuse to take the next major step.

I am thinking in particular of a friend who began his writing career by grinding out formulated plots for the pulp market. For those who are unaware of the term, "pulps" are sensationalized love or crime stories actually printed on a relatively cheap grade of paper stock known as "pulp." While many writers have launched illustrious careers by first writing for the pulps, some, like my friend, have never attempted to move on. For them, the pulp market represents "tested waters," a security blanket of sorts, while attempting another genre of writing is to once again risk rejection.

The problem with this kind of rationale is that my friend no longer feels creatively challenged by what he is doing. Meanwhile, lying in a dresser drawer is a rough draft of a screenplay he has been working on for several years. From what he has told me about it, I am inclined to believe it has merit. It certainly has an abundance of action and drama, and a powerfully uplifting message. But my friend has never attempted to tackle the movie business. To him, it is an "alien nation." Although there are many literary agents who specialize in this field, he is reluctant to approach any of them because of what he considers to be his "inferior credentials." And so, he continues along in the field he knows best, the one he no longer feels challenged by and secretly wishes to escape. Not surprisingly, he tends to identify with that particular brand of *unlucky* person who somehow just "never gets the breaks."

How can we know when we are operating above or below our own level of expertise? I suppose it is more of a "gut" feeling than anything else. I know that experiencing a struggle is not, in itself, a sign that we are "in over our heads." Hard work never hurt anyone. Then again, there is that feeling that life is not really *flowing*. Everything related to a given activity seems to lead to endless frustration and despair.

The *difficult* is *easier* for those with natural ability, which simply means that the success factor is essentially to be found in the ability of the doer. While latent abilities can certainly be developed, it would be unwise to depend upon an undeveloped ability to see you through a difficult or unfamiliar situation. The fact is, all too many people take disastrous "chances" by relying upon undeveloped abilities to accomplish their goals.

BEWARE OF THE LUCK-KILLER

Ah yes, there is always a villain in the piece! In this case, it is the dastardly luck-killer, whom so many fail to recognize because of his outwardly deceptive appearance. On the surface, he functions under the guise of confidence. Not only confidence—but *over*confidence!

The problem with overconfidence is that people are seldom aware when they are its victims. These are people who seek to mask their insecurities and lack of self-esteem by becoming reckless plungers. Their judgment is usually clouded by the need to demonstrate their extraordinary courage and daring. They talk constantly of having a "lucky feeling" which is nothing more than impulse growing out of inexperience. Overconfident people tend to underestimate the necessary requirements for success. They rush into investments, relationships and business dealings, never suspecting the hidden dangers involved until it is too late. Finding themselves totally unequipped to handle the obstacles that confront them, they later refer to the experience as "bad luck."

Through my own handicapping, I have become acquainted with dozens of successful individuals who make their living through pari-mutuel wagering. Contrary to common belief, the luckiest bettors never bet hunches or play impulsively. Behind the luck of the professional pari-mutuel wagerer are many hours of research, study and experience. The specialized knowledge of the "pro" has taught him to minimize risks by carefully evaluating them beforehand. Such expert gamblers study their craft just as stockbrokers, commodities and real estate brokers do. When they feel that they stand a good chance of matching their own ability to the inherent risks involved, they make their move.

HONESTY—STILL THE BEST POLICY

It always has been and always will be. The practice of honesty is of paramount importance in setting yourself up to attract good luck and good fortune. Unfortunately, many do not realize this, especially where money is concerned. Dishonest people consider themselves lucky regardless of the manner in which they manage to "win." To them, the true test of luck is material wealth. They generally justify their actions by insisting that it is a dog-eat-dog world, which, of course, makes it necessary for them to get whatever they can in order to survive. Nowadays, the tendency to employ dishonest tactics for purposes of personal gain is widespread.

While we all occasionally have dishonest thoughts, particularly when our minds are operating in the "survival" mode, it is foolish to believe that there is any long-range gain to be realized from behaving dishonestly.

Consider the life of a convicted bank robber. As a career criminal, he may have stolen many thousands of dollars from others but, in the end, he stole more from himself. What do you suppose he would now be willing to pay in order to regain his freedom? Undoubtedly, every cent he ever stole, and much more besides.

If you presently know dishonest individuals who seem to be "getting away with everything," perhaps you consider them lucky. We have all known people who appear to be living luxuriously while the rest of us work long and hard for what we have. What *do* we have? Better yet, what do the *others* have that we envy them for?

Every day that they live, dishonest people set themselves up for social, civil and criminal reproachment. Then too, they are often tormented in a psychological or spiritual way. Over a period of time, their dishonesty destroys their capacity for love and friendship because they believe there is no one they can really trust. Any person with a devious nature is certain to see others in a similar light. For that reason alone, they are not inclined to become close to anyone, which inevitably causes them to lead rather lonely and isolated lives.

Upon reconsideration, do you still feel that dishonest people have any real advantages? Or anything at ALL worth having? Wouldn't you rather sleep well at night? Wouldn't you rather be surrounded by loving family and friends, secure in the knowledge that you have no legitimate reason to be always looking over your shoulder?

See how lucky you are?

THE LINK BETWEEN CHANCE AND LUCK

We have talked about chance, and we have talked about luck. If, in the process, you have come to see one term as synonymous with the other, you will be surprised to learn that they are not.

The dictionary defines "chance" as a course of events not subject to calculation. Chance is comprised of an unpredictable number of happenings, both important and irrelevant. For the most part, it is best not to personalize them, or to respond to them in any significant way.

The link between "chance" and "luck" cannot occur until you develop an *emotional attachment* to a given situation or event. It is only then that chance becomes luck, since luck is really a *personalized perception of chance.*

For example, let us assume that you are an aspiring entrepreneur who has developed a new product that requires marketing and promotion. On impulse, you decide to attend a party, merely to enjoy an evening out. The dozens of people you mingle with play no significant role in your life, and so, your conversation is confined to "small talk." But then you chance to overhear a remark by a successful marketer who is looking for some new and exciting product to add to his line. Suddenly, "chance" takes on new meaning for you. What began as an impersonal remark now becomes extremely personal to you. And so, "chance" becomes "luck."

It is actually our RESPONSE mechanism to chance that determines our luck. As chances in life occur, they must first be recognized for what they are before anything more can be done. Or, to put it another way: *Observation is the key to transformation.*

Successful people have a talent for preparing themselves for chance. They know how to take advantage of it, while losers are only its victims.

You may have noticed that a victim of bad luck is generally a person who believes he is "jinxed" and that nothing good will ever happen to him. Would you say that he has been adversely affected by outside circumstances, or that outside circumstances have been allowed to adversely affect his thoughts? If you try to remind such a person that he has much to be grateful for, he will rarely, if ever, agree. Not unless he can be made to understand that he has NOT been singled out by external forces over which he has no personal control.

ACTIVELY CREATING GOOD LUCK

The truth is, we do not get what we want—*we get what we expect*. This is a basic fact of life. Before anything else can change, our expectation level must change from that of being a victim of life's misfortunes to being a receptor of opportunity. Accumulated evidence has shown that attitude is one of the most important factors in creating good luck. Through the right attitude, it is possible to develop the skill of *attracting* good luck with almost mathematical precision.

Since most misfortunes in life have their roots in faulty perceptions, it is in your own best interests to cultivate the most positive and constructive thoughts. Make no mistake about it! Your good luck is directly related to the information that is stored in that mental computer known as your subconscious mind. This information comes to you in a variety of ways—through other people, from things you read, from tapes you listen to, from what you see on television. And while there is certainly nothing wrong with being a good listener, observer or reader, great care must be taken to avoid the trap of merely "ingesting information" since that, in itself, will not insure success or good luck. Good luck and good fortune comes to those who are prepared to take some appropriate ACTION once an idea has been formed. Such people invariably find that the more action they take, the luckier they get!

POSITIVE EXPECTATION INCREASES GOOD LUCK

There are those who continue to take issue with the idea of "positive expectation," insisting that this encourages nothing more than false optimism. "I refuse to trick myself into believing things are better than they are!" such people will say.

To begin with, I would never encourage anyone to deliberately delude himself. On the other hand, there is nothing to be gained from looking at the negative side of life.

You may have heard it said that people who always expect the worst are seldom disappointed. Well, it's true! Such people have mastered the art of drawing negative situations into their lives through their own negative belief system and actions. How sad this is since it is just as easy, and certainly more advantageous, to remind yourself of the many legitimate reasons you have to be optimistic. Whatever the immediate problem, you can be sure that the solution is available to you, just waiting to be discovered. It will come to you when you are ready to accept it. This is what is meant by "positive expectation," and, believe me, it has nothing whatsoever to do with deluding yourself.

Immediate challenges and problems notwithstanding, it is important to remind yourself that you always possess the inner qualities and talents to turn the odds in your favor. So, forget about all the reasons why something may not work. You only need to find one good reason why it WILL!

A lucky person is one who recognizes chance opportunities, acts on them, and most of all—EXPECTS TO BE LUCKY!

CHAPTER 3
Probability Vs. Superstition

The terms "luck" and "superstition" seem to go hand in hand. Since most people do not know what luck actually is, or how to produce it in their lives, they tend to believe that luck is something that simply "happens" to them through some outside force. In an effort to influence this outside force in a positive way, man has created a number of "luck-producing" symbols. These include charms, four-leaf clovers, rabbit's feet, and many, many others. There are also *actions* that are felt to be luck-producing, such as knocking on wood, or tossing salt over one's shoulder. Most of these practices are cultural in nature, and none have any basis in fact.

Superstitions have existed since the beginning of time. From a belief in omens, superstitions have gradually developed through the ages, particularly on certain days. Consider the following examples:

The First of January—If, upon going to bed, a young woman drinks a pint of cold spring water that contains a mixture composed of the yolk of a pullet's egg, the legs of a spider, and the pounded skin of an eel, her future destiny will be revealed to her in a dream.

Valentine's Day—If the first person a single woman meets upon leaving her house early in the morning turns out to be a woman, she will not be married that year. If, on the other hand, she encounters a man, she will be married within three months.

St. Swithin's Eve—Decide upon three things you most wish to know and then write them down with a new pen and red ink on a sheet of finely woven paper, from which you have previously cut off and burned all four corners. Fold the paper into a lover's knot and wrap around it three hairs from your head. Place the paper under your pillow for three successive nights, and your curiosity to know the future will be satisfied.

If you find the foregoing superstitions little more than a laughing matter, consider this! A research project in which I was involved while studying psychology revealed that *83 percent of the participants* were superstitious! In one experiment, a large ladder was placed on the side of an office building on a busy downtown street. The ladder extended from the side of the building almost to the curb of the sidewalk. There was only a foot or so between the ladder and the curb but approximately ten feet *under* the ladder. No one was on the ladder and there was no activity going on in the immediate vicinity. Even so, 83 percent of a total of two thousand people made a point of walking around the ladder rather than under it! This clearly reveals that, at some level, many of us consider our luck to be tied to some invisible outside force.

Advanced scientific explanations have done little to dispel many of our irrational beliefs. Superstition tends to hang on like a cat with nine lives! In fact, according to a recent article dealing with the subject of psychic counseling (palm readers, psychics, channelers, astrologers, etc.), Americans spend over *eighteen million dollars annually* consulting with such practitioners.

While there appears to be some validity to the work performed by certain psychic counselors, the problem exists in separating the wheat from the chaff. The *real* danger, of course, lies in believing that there is something outside ourselves that determines our fate and fortune. The main point I am trying to make here is that we need to take a close look at anything and everything that encourages our dependency and *discourages* us from assuming personal responsibility for our lives.

WHY ARE WE SUPERSTITIOUS?

The wise philosopher Epicitus once said that "superstition comes from the *instinctive desire* to believe in casual relations which cannot be proved to exist through the course of reasoning or direct observation." In other words, superstition is one way of explaining the unexplainable, providing a reason (of sorts) for *why* things happen.

While superstition tends to vary from one religious, ethnic or occupational group to another, ALL groups seem to cling to these beliefs in negative situations.

How often have you heard someone say, "When your time comes, there is nothing you can do about it." Well, I guess there is some truth in this because, when you die, your time has certainly come!

The problem with superstition is that it tends to encourage us to *accept* and *adjust* to certain circumstances when we should actually be working at *changing* them. In the final analysis, it either becomes a matter of being "held prisoner" by your thoughts, or being freed and enlightened by them.

We all have our own inner hopes and fears which can be very firmly tied to our symbolic concepts of good and bad luck. What I want to impress upon you is that it is these concepts and beliefs that tend to activate the end result.

THE LAW OF PROBABILITY

According to well-known legal expert Sir William Blackstone, any "law" is a settled rule of action. The word itself suggests a desire for order, which people are constantly seeking in areas concerned with their thoughts, their emotions, health, financial affairs and all other phases of their life.

What we seek to uncover through the law of probability is yet another means of predicting events with some degree of accuracy. Probability evolves out of the use of mathematics, and also, our powers of observation. Although you may not be aware of it, you tend to predict events on almost a daily basis. For example, you might say, "I would really like to wash the car today, but it looks like rain." By simple observation, you have predicted the future. Because of some clouds in the sky, it appears there is a probability of rain, although it is hardly a certainty.

Some events happen so regularly that we can foretell them long before they actually occur. For example: the time of each sunrise and sunset, and the date of the next full moon. The changing of the seasons, while more subtly accomplished, nonetheless occurs at the same time every year.

During the seventeenth century, mathematics began to play an important role in helping to determine the likelihood of specific events. Because of his own interest in this field, British astronomer Edmund Halley was able to bring to an end many superstitions that had always clouded the minds of men. Up until then, people had believed that any unusual sighting in the sky was to be taken as a prediction of some forthcoming catastrophe. At such times, churches became extremely crowded, and priests would walk among the frightened people, giving them absolution for their sins.

In 1066, a great comet had been seen streaking across the sky. Halley decided to find out all he could about the appearance of such phenomena, in particular the years in which such comets were seen. He discovered that the cycles were about seventy-five years apart. Halley thought it unlikely that a number of different comets would appear at such regular intervals. His own feeling was that what people were actually seeing was the same comet over and over again. Halley predicted that the comet's next appearance would occur in 1959, and so it did. Since that time, it has continued to appear on a regular and totally predictable basis.

When seventeenth-century mathematicians began to study the law of probability, they centered their attentions upon coins and dice. They were primarily concerned with making accurate predictions of how a tossed coin or dice would land.

Since those early days, the law of probability has developed into an important branch of mathematics. At present, such studies are used in a variety of ways—in opinion polls, gambling odds, census taking, etc.

Have you ever given any thought to the manner in which insurance companies work with the law of probability? Consider the case of automobile insurance. Each year, policyholders pay specific amounts or premiums, in exchange for which they receive compensation for accidental losses. Insurance companies are able to secure enough income from premium payments and corporate investments to pay off such losses and still generate a profit. To determine how much to charge policyholders for such coverage, insurance companies study the law of probability to determine how many accidents are likely to occur within a given period. Unless their calculations are accurate, these companies will be forced to pay out more than they take in. In an effort to avoid this, they rely heavily upon *statistics*.

Statistics are actually a collection of information, involving figures, which help to answer the question of probability on any given subject. Whenever we study probability, it is important to remember that we can only work from *what we know*. Facts unknown to us can greatly affect the accuracy of any forecast, and frequently do. The more statistical information we have available to us, the better our chances of making accurate predictions.

Superstition, of course, is not based upon facts or statistics, which, in itself, makes it a totally unreliable tool for determining probability. On the other hand, reliable statistics, when combined with one's own mental powers, can certainly help us to work things out more favorably.

ODDS AND ENDS

What are your odds of achieving a certain end?

In order to be "lucky," it is necessary to come to terms with reality. Realistically speaking, your odds of winning a million-dollar lottery are about 125,000,000 to 1! You might wish to consider this when people say, "It only takes one ticket to win." That's right. The one *right* ticket out of a possible 125,000,000!

At this juncture, it might be reassuring to know that the odds against finding a pearl in an oyster are only 12,000 to 1.

Finally, if you toss a coin ten times, the odds that it will always come up heads are 1 in 1,023.

Where games of chance are concerned, many people can become severely disheartened by odds, and so, may decide to ignore them and keep hoping for a "lucky streak." It is an unfortunate decision at best, since luck is determined by probability over an extended period of time.

NOTE: Here again, it is important to remember the manner in which we were intended to use our own logic and intelligence.

The human mind is an organ over which man has a specific kind of control. Just as the driver of an automobile is capable of steering in a certain direction but cannot alter the mechanical laws by which the car functions, so too can he focus upon specific goals without measurably affecting the law of probability, which tends to dictate certain events.

Man is free to think or not to think. If he chooses *not* to think, or thinks unwisely, he will set into motion a complex chain of events that must inevitably bring about an unfortunate or undesired conclusion.

IGNORING PROBABILITIES— A LEARNED RESPONSE

When you were young, most likely you were not encouraged to consider the law of probability in that most children are taught to think in terms of *alternatives*.

"If you don't eat your supper, you can't have any dessert."

"You had better have this room cleaned up in an hour or we'll go to the movies without you."

When confronted with unpleasant alternatives, there is little to think about—or so it seems. Whatever is desired is obviously contingent upon something else. Do this and you get that. DON'T do this and you get THAT! There is nothing to ponder or research. It is an Either-Or situation.

Unfortunately, when this concept is carried over into adulthood, it frequently limits a person's outlook. He may continue to think purely on a level of punishment and reward, believing he will "win" if he is a good person who deserves to win. If he loses, he is obviously undeserving.

People who are locked into this view find it difficult to consider probabilities. They are also more likely to be superstitious since they tend to equate failure with something outside themselves. If you can be made to feel that you are a bad person and that only bad things will ever happen to you, you will tend to become highly superstitious where so-called "bad luck" is concerned. You will see it as a condition in life that deliberately seeks you out. It is your cross to bear. Whatever you do, you can never escape it. Anyone who attempts to show you the manner in which you are flagrantly ignoring the law of probability will be met with an attitude of "None of that stuff has anything to do with me. Lady Luck hasn't dealt me a decent hand since the day I was born. That's just the way it is."

However things are, it is important to remember that they could just as easily be some other way. You are *not* locked into any particular pattern of behavior or thought. Not unless you choose to believe you are!

BECOMING REALITY-BASED

By now, you undoubtedly understand, or have *begun* to understand, that you will never learn how to make *odds* or *probability* work in your favor until you are ready to accept the reality in every situation.

NOTE: Reality is not what you would like it to be, or someday *hope* it might be. It is what it is. Pure and simple. The nice thing about reality is that you DO have the choice of utilizing it in your own behalf. Of course, this will be difficult to do if you continue to confuse your personal preferences with what reality is all about. Please don't make the mistake of believing that reality is different things to different people. Reality simply is! It is only people's *perceptions* of reality that vary. You may be sure that your own perceptions will always be greatly influenced by whatever has happened to you in the past, what is happening now, and also, by what you would *like* to have happen.

EXAMPLE: Once you have become determined to win a million-dollar lottery, you will do whatever you feel is necessary in order to bring this happy experience about. In the process, you may well become a reckless plunger, but that will not change the odds (the reality) of the situation. Your chances of winning remain what they always were. You *may* win—but in all *probability*, you won't.

To become firmly anchored in reality is to automatically eliminate most of the problems you have in life. Why? Because most of them stem from your own inability (or unwillingness) to see what is really causing them. Yes, YOU are! Whatever you persist in accepting, believing, supporting, condoning, etc. is the REAL crux of the problem.

The first thing you should ask yourself is "Is it right?" Bear in mind that you only have one life to live. Can you think of any reason why you shouldn't constantly strive to make it the happiest, most productive life you possibly can? Is it wrong to be aware of the ways in which you are hurting yourself, or *allowing* yourself to be hurt? Is it wrong to try to change all that? If *you* don't, who will?

An unfortunate fact of life is that all too many people simply "wait" for things to get better. Although it tends to disturb them when nothing comes of this, it apparently doesn't disturb them enough. Change, when it finally occurs, is generally *forced* upon such people. When the negative aspects of their lives finally "back them into a corner," they may at last make some desperate move, one that is rarely if ever based on a logical decision.

Why is it that people wait so long to make a change? Why do they tend to *avoid* change? The one absolutely predictable thing in life is that circumstances will *always* change. For better. For worse. THINGS CHANGE. This is reality!

In order to live successfully, you will need to keep developing your coping skills in much the same way that a professional body-builder continues to develop his muscles. Remember! It is not what happens to you, but rather how well you *cope* with what happens, that will determine your success or failure in this world. And yes, it will be up to YOU to do it! Cease clinging to false hopes and nonsensical superstitions. Throw away that lucky rabbit's foot. It obviously didn't work for the rabbit! Heed the law of probability, and carefully weigh your options, evaluating them realistically—without adding any false assumptions and superstitions of your own.

Remember always that reality is what exists quite independent of our own minds and emotions. It cannot be colored by anything you think or feel. It IS what it IS and must be dealt with on those terms. Once you learn to fully accept this, you will find it much easier to work with the law of probability since you will then have ceased to fight against it. At this stage, you will no longer be tempted to bet on that long shot in the tenth race that would pay ninety-nine to one IF HE WINS! His breeding and past performance record clearly indicate that every other horse in the race would need to drop dead before THIS horse could win. *The statistics are there!* The odds are 99% against him. And no, it isn't going to help that he happens to have a "lucky-sounding" name!

On a more personal level, the same rules apply. You are NOT going to succeed in any job for which you have not been sufficiently trained, and no one else is going to solve your problems, change your life, or give you a million dollars. You are on your own!

Did you feel a little twinge of anxiety when you read that last line? Don't worry about it. Concentrate on becoming the best person you can possibly be and that feeling will eventually pass. The stronger, more knowledgeable and self-reliant you become, the less you will have to fear from *being on your own*. Once you have managed to become the one person in all the world you can truly depend upon, you will feel more secure than you have ever felt before.

PROBABILITY THINKING— HOW IT WILL HELP YOU TO GROW

Once you have become a true advocate of the law of probability, you may notice some interesting changes taking place. These inner changes will gradually cause you to develop an entirely new attitude toward everything you think and do.

For one thing, you will develop a much more methodical approach to complex tasks. This may astound you at first, particularly if you have always been an impatient or impulsive person. You may find that you have suddenly developed an interest in books, and that you now have an eye for detail, and some newly acquired skills for cataloguing, filing and classifying materials according to content and relevance. In time, you will begin to realize that you are becoming an Accurate Thinker, someone whose heightened curiosity, persistence and intellectual attributes are finally being put to good use.

Much to your own amazement, you will notice that other, more "reckless" types can no longer persuade you to act unwisely. High-pressure salesmen who urge you to make a buying decision "Now—TODAY!" will have suddenly lost their intimidating influence. Friends or family members who have always been able to threaten or cajole you into doing things you would rather not do, will have to take a backseat to your own "better judgment" which is now determined to weigh all the pros and cons before any final decisions are made. You will fare much better in personal relationships, realizing now that love and respect are not favors to be automatically bestowed. If you feel that others do not yet regard you as you would LIKE to be regarded, in all *probability*, you have not yet earned their affection or respect. Instead of vigorously *opposing* this thought, you will find you are now able to deal with it, and will begin at once to make some constructive changes.

You will develop a greater respect for the infallibility of mathematics, particularly as it assists you in achieving the most practical and desired outcome.

All-in-all, you will adopt a much calmer, more reasonable approach to daily challenges, and the benefits of this will be obvious, and far-reaching.

No longer willing to leave things "to chance," you will see how advanced knowledge, when carefully and studiously applied, can attract the "good luck" that has always eluded you. *It was there all the time.* You can BET on it!

CHAPTER 4
The Ebb and Flow Of Chance

It is important to realize that everything in the universe is in balance. Were this not so, planets would collide, and the oceans would devour the earth. There would be no seasons of the year, no vegetation or animal life, no air to breathe. Quite simply, if things were not in balance, nothing would even *be*!

By the same token, the meanings of words would become extremely difficult to comprehend. Consider such words as health, happiness, fame and fortune. The only real way to understand and appreciate such words is through some opposite point of reference. If there were no opposite to happiness, what would happiness actually mean? The same holds true for wealth. Its opposite is poverty, and it is the poverty side of things that makes it possible for us to truly appreciate a life of ease.

Do you think it is merely coincidence that some opposite for everything exists? Imagine living in a state of perpetual happiness. Do you think it would eventually exhaust you? Do you think it might make you somewhat callous toward the misfortunes of others? Do you think you would begin to take happiness for granted?

The fact is, unless there is an opposite to balance things out, it is impossible to live realistically, or with any true sense of values.

This chapter is about the Ebb and Flow of Chance, and why it works as it does. Given a choice in the matter, we would undoubtedly prefer to have luck always on our side, just as we would prefer to have happiness, good health, and financial comfort. Still, chance has its own rhythm, and the difference between so-called "lucky" people and "unlucky" ones is that those who are lucky have come to understand this incredible flow of activity and action.

While there is no way of knowing when favorable chances are apt to enter our lives, the more we know about chance and how it works, the greater the likelihood of recognizing favorable conditions and converting them into good luck.

Our lives are filled with chance situations that constantly require us to make some personal decisions. Many chances that look promising on the surface can bring misfortune if acted upon in a rash or impulsive manner. Then too, there are chances that can bring good luck and good fortune to one person, and bad luck and misfortune to another. Given the many choices in life, we must train ourselves to recognize those that are truly beneficial, and those that are not. Successful recognition is the first step toward a life filled with "lucky" or desirable results.

STAYING ON THE ALERT

The psychological basis for recognizing opportunity is alertness. It is important to always be attuned to significant "turning points," the kind that provide the most fortuitous combination of people, circumstances and information. How do you do this? By recognizing and acting upon the "flow of opportunity" when it comes into your life, and by cautiously holding back when you find yourself in the "ebb" or downside of this same rhythmic pattern. Go with the flow, and luck will be yours! Miss it, and you miss the chance for fulfilling your desires until the tide again turns in your favor.

In speaking with highly creative people, I have invariably found that they are closely attuned to their creative highs and lows, and have learned to function well in either state.

For instance, as a writer, the worst thing I can possibly do is to try to force the words out of my head and onto the paper. There are days when I find it difficult to write. If I force the words, they just don't flow. It's like jamming a computer. On such, days, I find it is best not to write at all.

Still, I have learned that during this creative "ebb" period, I can do other related tasks that keep me on track until the flow returns. Such things include:

1. Editing
2. Rewriting
3. Organizing material
4. Reading books on the subject I am writing about
5. Jotting down new ideas on 3 × 5 cards
6. Talking to individuals or brainstorming with them for the purpose of stimulating new creative ideas

Taking advantage of my creative ebb, I still manage to accomplish a great deal, and all of it has some significant bearing on the end result.

Moral of the Story: When we talk about the ebb and flow of opportunity, we are not necessarily talking in monetary terms. The really important thing is to make each period work for you in the best possible way!

RIDING THE TIDE

Coming to terms with the Ebb and Flow of Chance is clearly a matter of understanding. The thing you must understand is this: *No matter how low the ebb, a favoring chance at opportunity is just around the corner.*

Do you doubt it? Then look back over your life and see if you can honestly say that things have always been bad for you, that nothing good has ever happened since the day that you were born.

I know without even asking, without even meeting you, that you have had your share of peaks and valleys. It may seem to you that the bad has greatly outweighed the good, but that is only because the good is often taken for granted. Isn't it true that we tend to take good health for granted—until we no longer have it? And what of the fact that we have roofs over our heads, and food to eat, and a job to go to everyday? Do you know of anyone who makes a deliberate effort to give daily thanks for such blessings? If so, that is a rare individual indeed. Most people accept such things as their due. In truth, they would like to have MORE. This is altogether normal—unless "having more" becomes the primary objective in life. Once it does, it creates a whole new set of problems, which will be discussed a little later on in this chapter.

WAITING FOR THE TIDE TO TURN

Your psychological disposition plays an important role in your recognition of the flow of opportunity. What is your attitude toward the "ebb" while you are out of the flow? Do you find constructive things to do while you are waiting for the tide to turn, or do you just sit around, feeling sorry for yourself, hoping and wishing things will change?

To be a Winner it is necessary to turn your mind away from self-doubt, disappointment and self-pity, and become mentally, physically, psychologically and spiritually *receptive* to a new inflow of opportunity so that you will be *ready* when it comes.

Before you can measurably increase your good luck and good fortune, there is one basic truth you MUST come to terms with: *There is no way that you can constantly lose if you think like a Winner.* By maintaining a consistently high level of alertness while things are not going well, you will sense when there is a shift from ebb to flow. Sometimes the shift will occur slowly. At other times, it will hit with the force of a lightning bolt!

It can all begin with an *idea*! It may well be a professionally oriented idea, or one connected with health, finances or personal relationships. Behind such ideas you may be sure there is the power to make some incredible changes which, in turn, will draw all the right people, conditions and circumstances into your life. That is *one* way in which a sudden shift from ebb to flow can work.

On the negative side, you may choose instead to weaken your position by allowing past misfortunes to make you feel victimized or doubtful. In that case, you will tend to draw *additional* misfortune, and so, the negative cycle will continue.

ARE YOU MYTHING OUT ON LIFE?

Perhaps you are, if you have chosen to believe such erroneous assumptions as "opportunity knocks only once." This, like so many other myths, has its basis in false perception. Opportunity *constantly* presents itself, but unless you have a true clarity of purpose, you will fail to recognize it, and so, will not take the appropriate action.

Since one person may want what another casts aside, it is extremely important to understand what it is you are looking for. Understanding your true desires is the key to recognizing favorable circumstances and extracting the greatest amount of good luck from them. By carefully calculating your chances against your desires, you can accurately determine where luck exists and where it does not.

Most people equate good luck with the experience of a sudden financial windfall. Winning a million-dollar lottery is certainly considered lucky! But suppose you are already a millionaire with an incurable disease. Would winning another million dollars make you feel lucky? Probably not. You would feel a lot luckier if you heard of a new medical breakthrough that offered a possible cure for your disease.

In the final analysis, luck is really a matter of personal perception. Now and again, you may have heard someone say, "I consider myself lucky if I just make it through the day." Admittedly, this is not a person with extremely high aspirations, but such people certainly exist.

THE NUMBER ONE LUCK KILLER

Sometimes our desires are not in keeping with what is best for us. Before we act on any desire, we should always examine that desire in terms of its true benefits.

The number one luck killer is psychological addiction! Addiction is simply the uncontrollable, neurotic desire for something we feel we MUST HAVE in order to feel complete. Once this addictive desire becomes our master, it will quickly pave the way for failure, or even self-destruction.

Before you allow yourself to believe that there is something—*anything*—you simply MUST HAVE, ask yourself, "Is this going to add to my life in some truly beneficial way, or is it only satisfying a neurotic need that will eventually create additional problems?"

Every desire needs to be carefully examined and understood in that light.

Some people have uncontrolled, excessive desires that cause

them to live in a state of perpetual anxiety. Regardless of their immediate station in life, they always feel inferior to something or someone else. No matter how much they already have, or how much they have accomplished, there remains the neurotic desire to have MORE.

WANT VS. ADDICTION

While it is certainly normal to *want* something, it is NOT normal to *need* it to a point where we literally become *addicted* to having it. Addiction is a sign of low self-esteem which usually manifests in childhood, out of a sense of inadequacy. Most things addicts are addicted to are replacements for whatever they feel they lack. In later years the addict tries to compensate for his feelings of inadequacy by becoming neurotically obsessed with having something or someone to make him feel "okay" about himself.

There are many forms of socially unacceptable addictions such as drugs, alcohol and sex. There are some addictions that are equally as neurotic and destructive but are more socially acceptable. An example is the "Wealth Addiction."

The wealth addict is neurotically obsessed with acquiring money which he hopes will compensate for his emotional insecurity. Once money has become the primary focus, the wealth addict may willingly sacrifice family, friends, loving relationships, even personal health and well-being in an effort to satisfy his emotional needs.

The wealth addict, like any other addict, is rarely inclined to ask himself if he can *afford* his addiction. Whatever the price, the end result seems somehow justified. Since the wealth addict tends to equate money with happiness, he is often attracted to a variety of poorly thought-out schemes in his effort to make a quick buck. Because of this, he will generally suffer at the hands of his own poor judgment. The wealth addict invariably ends up with quite the reverse of what he had hoped to achieve.

Unfortunately, the wealth addict has a habit of passing on his own false sense of values to others. His children tend to become typical "yuppies" who permit their own desires and personal philosophies to be dictated by the advertising media. Not only must such people have everything they see, but they must have it NOW!

Having placed themselves under incredible pressure, wealth addicts and their offspring are determined to achieve the happiness, contentment and personal fulfillment they feel can only come from possessing everything there is. More is never enough for any addict.

Addicts are Losers. On the surface they look like Winners, but in actuality, they fit the Loser profile and live a Loser life-script. On the other hand, Winners realize that it is one thing to be motivated to fulfill a desire, and quite another thing to be obsessed with it! They seek to gratify their wants on a basic, nonaddictive level.

THE OTHER SIDE OF THE COIN

It should be noted that it is no less addictive or self-destructive to constantly repress normal, natural desires. Some people do not allow their desires to surface because they feel they are incapable of fulfilling them. By refusing to admit what they want, they believe that it is possible to avoid the disappointment associated with not achieving their goals. Such people, as Thoreau states, tend to lead lives of "quiet desperation" which is all that can ever result from not fulfilling their natural desires.

LEARNING TO BECOME EBB-ULLIENT

Those possessed with ebullience are those who have a certain quality of enthusiastic expression. In the course of writing this book, it occurred to me that someone who has mastered the art of living successfully through "ebb" times might well be described as *ebb*-ullient. According to my own definition, rather than Webster's, this would be a person who demonstrates a certain quality of enthusiastic expression during "low" times. Refusing to be discouraged or disconcerted by sudden changes in luck, an ebb-ullient person would be more inclined to utilize such times in the most positive and productive ways.

What should you do when things stop working for you, when you seem to be stuck in a rut, or when you are living in limbo? What CAN you do?

You might begin by indulging in a few moments of silent reflection. Better yet, let's decide on a definite length of time. *Fifteen minutes of silent reflection.* During this period, you should simply allow your mind to wander wherever it will. Don't be surprised if it begins to cultivate a lot of new ideas. You can be sure that they have been there all along. It's just that you have never before taken the time to acknowledge them.

After fifteen minutes of silent reflection, you might suddenly find yourself ready to make a list of fifteen positive things you can accomplish during the next week. Let's take a moment to consider what these might be:

1. Develop a natural offshoot to the business I am presently engaged in to carry me through slow times.
2. Make new business contacts.
3. Brainstorm with those in a similar or related field.
4. Practice thinking BIG! Write myself a check for a sizable amount and make a point of looking at it every day. Imagine really HAVING this money in my bank account as a result of something I have accomplished.
5. Read books and listen to cassette tapes on the subjects of self-motivation and self-improvement. Do this first thing every morning—last thing every night.

(NOTE: Can you think of another ten things to do during slow or "ebb" times that will help you restore your confidence and enthusiasm? Give it a try. The object is to make this a regular habit, so that ebb times will no longer affect you in a negative way.)

6.

7.

8.

9.

10.

11.

12.

13.

14.

15.

If you had trouble with this list, you may already sense that the trouble is *not* with the list. There is much to do and to think about, as this list will readily prove.

Another list it would be wise to make during "ebb" times is one that itemizes various things that make you feel good and lift your spirits. Your subconscious mind will automatically react to this positive stimulus, causing you to think and feel as you did when everything was going well. This is a powerful incentive and one that is guaranteed to work! By way of example:

Some years ago, I spoke with a topflight straight-commissioned salesman who was experiencing a temporary "slump." He was concerned about his poor volume of sales since he had no draw or guaranteed salary to sustain him throughout this time. For the most part, he preferred it that way, knowing that a guarantee could easily become a comfortable little cushion to fall back on.

"If I know there will be two thousand dollars coming in every month, there is the automatic temptation to live within these bounds," he explained. "As it is, I can earn as much as I want. In other words, the sky's the limit!"

While I could certainly understand his rationale on the "up" side, I asked him how well he was able to cope with the "down" side, which is the inevitable opposite to periods of peak production.

"That *has* been a problem," he admitted. "For one thing, I tend to chastise myself for not anticipating such times, for not managing my life in a truly professional way. Unfortunately, this hasn't accomplished much. In fact, it only makes me feel worse."

"I'm sure it does," I said. "And that may be the real problem." At this point, I made the following suggestion. "The next time you find yourself in a slump, instead of asking yourself what you are doing wrong, ask yourself what you were doing when you were doing it *right!*"

The salesman's eyes immediately brightened. "Why, I can answer that right now! Only last month, I was the top producer for the company. I've got to admit that a few of my prospecting techniques were pretty new and innovative. I remember that..."

As I listened, I watched a salesman-in-a-slump turn back into a topflight producer, and all because he had suddenly learned how to live through "ebb" times in the most positive and productive way.

It helps to realize that the peaks and valleys in your life are equally important to your overall success and well-being. Now and again, we need time to regroup. This was really driven home to me one day when I happened to overhear a conversation in a restaurant. Two women were seated in a booth close to mine. They were both smartly dressed, with an aura of true professionalism about them. Still, there was something a bit harried and harassed about them too, as if the pressures of daily life were beginning to wear them down.

At one point in their conversation, one of the women said: "The real problem is, you never have time to THINK!"

While such a statement may appear to be something of an exaggeration, it is, in fact, a surprisingly accurate definition of daily life. Consider it in the context of what goes on from the time you first wake up in the morning. Perhaps you wake up to an alarm. You hear it go off and jump out of bed. From that moment on, you undertake a series of ritualistic activities associated with preparing yourself for another day. You shower and dress. You eat breakfast. You jump into the car and drive to work. Once you arrive, there is yet another schedule to be observed. Everything is pretty systematic and more or less predetermined. At the end of the day, there is rush hour traffic to contend with, dinner to be eaten, a few things to be done around the house. There is an hour or two of family time, and then it is time for bed.

In reflecting upon such a daily routine, how much time would you say is actually given over to any form of creative or independent thought? That's the whole problem, you see! There is so little opportunity to THINK!

But what if you *did* have time to think? Do you suppose you would realize that you do not really like the job you are going to each day, and that it is time for a change? Do you think you might be able to map out some new strategy for living a better life, for achieving some long-forgotten goals, for turning a favorite hobby into a truly profitable endeavor? It all takes thought. If you only had time to *think*!

Had it ever occurred to you that this might be what "ebb" times are for? Once you begin to see them in that light, you will begin to appreciate them, to actually be grateful for them! The fact is, these are not really fallow periods, not unless you allow them to be.

YOUR SILENT PARTNER

The powerful forces of the subconscious mind, like all other great natural forces, can be harnessed and placed into service— by YOU! But before this can be done, it is first necessary to understand just what these forces are, how they work, and the best ways in which to utilize them.

The average person employs less than 25 percent of his or her subconscious power. It is indeed unfortunate that we allocate so little time to "going within," since there are tremendous resources waiting there, just waiting to be used! Can you afford to ignore them, to continue along as before, with this incredible giant sleeping inside you?

Think about it the next time you have time to THINK—during ebb times when nothing seems to be going your way.

Don't allow yourself to become discouraged or defeated.

Instead, be EBB-ullient!

CHAPTER 5
How Others Influence Your Win Factor

In the course of researching this book, I conducted hundreds of interviews with people who believed themselves to be "lucky." An analysis of their responses led me to conclude that there was one significant thread running through the lives of ALL lucky people. The one very obvious thing that they all had in common was that they were *curious* people.

The curious personality is one that is open to all new relationships, circumstances and events. Not surprisingly, over half the people interviewed admitted that their luck had changed dramatically because of individuals that they happened to meet by "chance."

In the course of attracting good luck and good fortune, it is extremely important to focus on this helpful information since most of our good luck will come to us through other people. Does this mean that everyone we meet is destined to have a beneficient effect upon our lives? *Hardly!* Perhaps only one in a hundred people will actually influence our good luck and good fortune, but the important thing is to remain *open* to this possibility!

EXPANDING YOUR VIEW

Increasing your win factor involves exposing yourself to new relationships, ones that are happy, healthy and positive in nature.

Does the foregoing accurately describe the people you are presently associating with? How would you rate these people in terms
of optimism and success? Remember! There is a natural tendency
to emulate those we constantly surround ourselves with.

While close friends and family members certainly play an important role in determining our good luck and good fortune, the
most *promising* influence will usually come from strangers, or
from people we hardly know. The reason for this is that, over a
period of time, friends and family tend to "settle in" to their
comfortable little niches, and so, seldom have new and stimulating ideas or experiences to share. This is not to say that such
relationships are not significant but rather that, in the context
of increasing our luck potential, they are less likely to stimulate
us in the proper ways.

The magical power of curiosity should never be underestimated.
The curious person is generally somewhat adventurous, which
automatically increases his or her potential for encountering more
favorable "chances" in life.

The immediate reward to be gained from meeting new people
and listening to their success stories is that this will motivate
you to be more positive, more adventurous in your *own* life. As
you listen to such people, you may hear only a sentence or two
that is actually capable of altering your limited views or perceptions, but this is all that is needed!

UNLIMITED THINKING
INCREASES CREATIVITY

Once you find yourself surrounded by the *right* people, you will
automatically begin to expand your horizons. There will be a
tendency to allow yourself to engage in *unlimited thinking*, which
simply means that you have chosen to lay immediate obstacles
aside and are now focusing on the end result. Unlimited thinking
enables you to get in touch with the "big picture" which, in itself,
is so essential to your success. Why? Because *all great works begin
with great vision!*

In the course of associating with unlimited thinkers, you may
uncover a somewhat distrubing truth about yourself. Think back
for a moment (perhaps to your high school or college days), when

someone you knew and admired was voted "most likely to succeed." In later years, you were probably not surprised if this person did, in fact, live up to every good thing that had ever been said about him or her. The reason for this is that it is relatively easy for us to have great visions about others, but what of the vision we hold of ourselves?

If you have children, notice how frequently you engage in the process of unlimited thinking for *them*! I'm sure you often think about their future and all the wonderful paths they may take.

In romantic relationships, it is also not uncommon to endow your loved one with unlimited potential. After all, this is the person of your dreams!

But what about *you*? If you find that you tend to see yourself and your own potential in a far more limited light, you have just uncovered the best possible reason for bringing some unlimited thinkers into your life. *What they KNOW they can SHOW!* Among other things, they will show you how to develop a far better image of yourself, how to recognize your TRUE potential, how to be the best possible YOU!

You may be sure that a large portion of your negative ideas came from people whose own inner doubts and fears were responsible for amplifying your own. Consider a situation in which you are having money problems. A negative-thinking individual would be the first to commiserate, to share with you all the financial reversals that he himself has experienced. Over a period of time, the constant fears and struggles of others tend to cast doubt upon your own abilities to prosper. This is especially true if you have fallen into the habit of believing that these "other" people are smarter or more resourceful than you. If you truly believe this, you will tend to focus on your fears rather than on possible solutions to your problem.

The negative influence of others can also be extended to the collective thoughts of *many* people. Make no mistake about it! Large groups generate *powerful thought patterns* that may adversely affect your own thinking. A good example of this is the news media, which is constantly bombarding us with talk about recessions, depressions or some other potentially catastrophic event. Economic downturns often make people feel that everything is "out of control" when, in fact, these times are only counterbalances to more prosperous times. What's more, economic downturns are inevitable. That being the case, you must decide for yourself if you are going to exist in perpetually "troubled times" or in a world of never-ending opportunity. It might interest you to know that many positive-thinking individuals actually prospered during the Great Depression. It is all a matter of individual perception, and also, a matter of not allowing yourself to get caught in a trap of accepting someone else's thoughts, ideas or feelings as your own.

HOW TO RECOGNIZE THOSE THAT CAN INFLUENCE YOUR WIN FACTOR

Winners attract good luck by recognizing and acting upon their own inherent characteristics and abilities. They do not dedicate themselves to anything that others think they should do or be. Rather, they allow themselves to follow their own inner promptings. Winners may occasionally lose ground, but they never lose the battle. Through it all, they hold fast to their own self-confidence and self-esteem. In all circumstances, under all conditions, they are not afraid to use their own self-knowledge and to do their own thinking. They separate facts from opinions and come to their own conclusions. While they do not pretend to have all the answers, they are not inclined to play the "helpless little victim" role. Nor do they blame others for their so-called "bad luck."

Winners have an inner sense of timing that works to their advantage. They know when it is time to be assertive and when it is time to be passive. They also know there is a time to work and a time to play, a time to speak and a time to be silent, a time to be sociable and a time to be alone. Quite simply, winners know that time is their most precious commodity, and rather than wasting it, they always use it in the most positive and productive ways.

Although they live in the moment and thoroughly enjoy life, winners have learned to postpone or delay gratification, which losers generally find it impossible to do.

Winners are able to make a successful transition from childhood to adulthood, from helplessness to independence. Notwithstanding the fact that they once depended upon others for food, clothing and shelter, they are eager to assume responsibility for obtaining such things for themselves.

As mature individuals, Winners know that they can set themselves up to win or to lose, and that personal attitude plays a major role in their lives. For that reason alone, Winners live in a state of *positive expectancy*. They expect to win, and that is one of the reasons they DO!

Faith also plays an important role in a Winner's life. Faith is a belief that there is something higher, greater and much more powerful that we can call upon to awaken us to positive chances for good luck and good fortune. As we become more conscious and aware, we automatically begin to make better choices. When we expect to win, and then add faith to our expectations, we begin to accept winning as a natural and inevitable event.

Such is the character of Winners! Without doubt, such people can have a powerful influence upon your life. But so can losers!

HOW TO RECOGNIZE THOSE THAT CAN INFLUENCE YOUR LOSS FACTOR

The unfortunate thing about Losers is that they often approach us in disguise. Notwithstanding their own inability to win, they often create a "facade of success" with which they hope to impress others.

Have you ever known anyone who professes to be an "expert" on matters that interest you? You should know at the outset that true Winners do not think of themselves as experts. For them, living and learning is an ongoing process. But Losers like to feel they have "arrived." They also like to convince others of it, and masquerading as an expert is one way in which they attempt to do this.

What can you learn from an pseudo "expert"? Usually, all the reasons why something is impractical or impossible to do. Avoid "pseudo-experts" (not to be confused with highly experienced and knowledgeable people who stand ready and willing to assist you in whatever way they can). It may take you a while to see through this particular disguise, but in time, it will become second nature.

Another way in which a Loser may disguise himself is through the *suggestion of wealth*. "Keeping up with the Joneses" is part of what this masquerade is all about. Living in a house you can't afford, driving a car it is breaking your back to buy insurance and license plates for, being seen in all the "right" places and paying exorbitant fees for the privilege. This is what status-conscious Losers often feel compelled to do. It is indeed unfortunate that so many others are suckered into their fraudulent life-style, actually *envying* these people for what they appear to have. What DO they have? Basically, a high-pressure, stress-filled life that is almost certain to drive them to an early grave.

In addition to the foregoing examples, Losers have many other ways of disguising themselves. Sometimes they do it through Size and Volume. I have known a few corporate executive types who were extremely intimidating to their subordinates because of their tall, portly appearance, and because they always spoke in a loud, booming voice. I have also known people who compensated for a *lack* of height by placing the desk in their office on a small podium. In front of the desk there could usually be found a velvet couch which was specifically designed for "sinking into." Imagine how it might feel to talk with a tall, fat, loudly demonstrative "boss" while you were sitting on a piece of furniture that gave you the sensation of having fallen down a hole. How would you feel about asking for a promotion and a raise in such a setting? How well do you think you would be able to debate an issue or defend a moral principle?

Oddly enough, the really great intimidators of this world tend to feel even less secure than the people they are constantly intimidating. That is their main reason for wanting power and control in every situation. Intimidators believe that whatever they don't control, controls them. And perhaps they are right. If they tend to be drawn to others like themselves (which is often the case), everybody is sure to be playing the same game.

Another Loser type you should make it a point to avoid is the Ego Tripper. This person rarely, if ever, wears a disguise since he is so insanely proud of WHO and WHAT he thinks he is! Ego Trippers generally make a point of bending your ear on how well they have their "act together." They always talk in terms of mega-bucks, and are constantly working on the biggest deal that ever was! They are name droppers, of course, and will try to impress you with their original paintings, with the labels on their suits—with everything they own and everyone they know. Are you impressed? NO? Good! That means you haven't been taken in by yet another kind of Loser.

Loser types come in so many different varieties that it would be virtually impossible to list them all. Even so, it is essential that you recognize them, which you will gradually learn to do, given enough time and practice.

Do you presently have any unpaid negative advisors in your life? These are people who are in the habit of criticizing your ideas and undermining your dreams. To hear them tell it, everything has already been tried. If others couldn't do it, then neither can you. If allowed to, carpers and harassers will happily become self-appointed guardians of your life. The object, of course, is to see to it that you are as firmly entrenched in a rut of frustration and hopelessness as *they* are. Watch out for such people! They too are Losers.

Do you know anyone who is particularly adept at making you feel guilty about "striking out on your own"? Such people will frequently remind you that since you have certain obligations and responsibilities in life, you can hardly afford to go off on some tangent. To their way of thinking, a steady salary is obviously what is needed to insure the comfort and security of those you love. In this, we have yet another Loser philosophy. Where is it written that you can't gradually phase yourself into a new career as you continue to work at something that provides the basic essentials of life?

IF OTHERS THINK YOU'RE CRAZY, MAYBE YOU'RE FINALLY GOING SANE

The real problem with irrational arguments is that they eventually begin to make sense. If you persist in carrying on relationships with people who have branded you "a little crazy" (simply because they cannot identify with your desires or dreams), look out! Such people are usually the majority. This, of course, has nothing to do with the fact that they are "right." It just happens that there are a lot more people who do NOT pursue their dreams than people who DO. But you already *know* that, right? Then how can these people possibly dissuade you from achieving your goals? Believe me, they CAN! And they have a number of insidious ways of going about it.

For one thing, their arguments may not be logical, but they are repetitive. For as long as there is an audience available, these Loser types will continue to "harp on the same old string" until they finally wear you down. Don't say it can't happen! It can happen on a day when you are feeling a little depressed, a little under-the-weather, a little more vulnerable than usual. On such days, you should *never, never* expose yourself to the negativities of others. If you happen to find yourself stuck with one of these Losers in a work environment, or any other environment from which you cannot immediately escape, then terminate the conversation, or tune these people out! There is always *something* you can do to maintain your equilibrium, to keep yourself in a positive frame of mind when everything around you seems hopelessly negative.

Think forward to a day when all these same "gloom-and-doomers" will be patting you on the back, insisting that they "always *knew* you could do it!" I promise you that such a day will come, and when it does, you will have mixed emotions. On the one hand, you will feel good about having proven yourself. Then again, you may feel resentful toward those who were not generous or gracious enough to provide their moral support when you needed it the most. Whatever feelings you may experience, I urge you not to fight them. Allow yourself to feel whatever you feel, then lay the matter aside. Not just for an hour or a day—but *forever*! Take comfort in the fact that you have managed to escape the bonds that still imprison so many others who have never dared to dream or ACT! Their lives are over while yours is just beginning!

POSSIBILITIES VS. LIABILITIES

One of the major differences between Winners and Losers is the way in which they view their own life situations. NOTE: You can expect people to influence YOUR life in much the same way that they influence their own lives. Here again, we have a strong argument for seeking out only those people who are capable of influencing your "win factor" in a truly positive way.

You will immediately recognize a Winner as someone who is constantly concerned with *possibilities*. Losers, on the other hand, tend to be preoccupied with *liabilities*. Winners always have a realistic attitude toward what is involved. They will be quick to remind you that no one ever said it was easy or safe. It isn't! Why SHOULD it be? We are not here simply to avoid pain and to enjoy pleasure. We are here for a purpose—to accomplish our life's work, to realize our true potential! And yes, there is a price tag attached. Winners are willing to pay that price in the interests of living life as it was *meant* to be lived.

"You win if the music is played according to your beat," a Winner will say. "You lose, if it isn't."

Japanese philosopher Suzuki may have said it best: "*I am an artist at living,*" he once observed, "*and my work of art is my life.*"

What IS your life?

If you were to ask a lot of different people that question, the answers would probably astound you. The really astounding thing is that the answers themselves are so *narrow*. The reason for this is that we tend to equate our lives with whatever primarily dominates them.

"My *work* is my life" is a typical answer. "My family and home" is another. What is interesting about these answers is the tenacious tone in which they are invariably voiced. It is as if the person speaking were actually more *determined* to see life through than actually to experience and enjoy it.

Life was not meant to be a task! It was meant to be a period of constant discovery, a constant unfolding, even as the petals of a flower unfold and open themselves to the sun. Can you envision your life in these terms? If not, is it because your life has become so routinely structured that there is nothing left to anticipate or enjoy?

Perhaps you have stopped trying to win, have simply resigned yourself to existing. Like a sentence to be served until your death. What grim thoughts on such a bright and sunny day! Had you even noticed what kind of day it was? Why don't you do that right now? Open the door and look outside. Does the day hold promise or only problems? *Possibilities* or *liabilities*? What will the mail bring—good news or bad? What will you do about it when it comes?

Try for a moment to see the day objectively, outside the realm of your own immediate thoughts and feelings. Take note of the reality that IS, the way it might appear to an alien being who had just landed on earth. Such a creature would not see things in terms of what he "expected the day to be like." His views and impressions would not be hopelessly clouded by the thought of having to fight traffic on the freeway, of having a tax bill to pay, of facing the threat of being demoted in his job. He would simply look and observe what lay in front of him. Just as Winners do! Possibilities. Possibilities everywhere! A day of promise. A sprinkle of gold dust in the air!

Are you sure it is NOT that kind of day? Perhaps it *is*, and you have merely failed to see it. SEE it for once, and RESPOND to what you see! Consider the fact that there might actually be some wonderful things waiting to happen to you today. Happy little surprises you hadn't really expected or counted on. Remember! We don't get what we want, *we get what we expect*!

One of the interviews I conducted while writing this book was with a woman who was kind enough to share some childhood reminiscences.

"It was during World War II," she told me. "My parents ran a boarding house. The mood in that house was always directly affected by the number of vacant rooms we had. Times were hard and we needed every cent that the rent from boarders could bring. Late at night, it was not uncommon for me to suddenly 'fall awake' and hear the voices of my parents in another room. I would listen as they discussed the unpaid bills, and all the dreadful things that would undoubtedly happen to us. I could never bear to hear this last part, and would bury my head in my pillow rather than hear that we were to be tossed out into the snow. Interestingly enough, it never quite came to that, and we always managed to survive.

"During that period, there is one part of my life that stands out more vividly than the rest, perhaps because it was so uncharacteristically cheerful. It concerned itself with one of our female boarders, a young woman who worked in a local defense plant. She was dating an older man, someone I remember only as Jerry. Jerry was a nightclub singer who frequently entertained us with his lovely Irish tenor voice. The thing I particularly remember about him is that he always came into our house singing. On the worst of all possible days, when it seemed that there might not be enough money to buy another load of coal for the furnace, Jerry would suddenly come through the door, singing the most popular tune of the day. All in a moment, the somber bleakness of our lives would be swept away. I would find myself laughing and dancing with him. I never wanted him to leave. I imagined myself in love with him. For me, he represented all that life could ever be."

Not only *could* be, but obviously was, at least while Jerry was there. This story is interesting because of what Jerry actually represented. He was certainly more than just a person to this frightened little girl whose life had been adversely affected by poverty and war. He was the other side of the coin, the hope and promise of a better and brighter tomorrow.

INFLUENCING YOUR OWN WIN FACTOR

Throughout your life there will be many Winners like Jerry who will do much to brighten your spirits, to point you in the right direction, and to give you the benefit of their knowledge and experience.

On the other hand, there will be many Losers who will do their level best to influence your life in a negative way. The answer lies in the choices we make. Remember! Your Win Factor is profoundly influenced by the company you keep. Part of betting on yourself is decreasing your association with Losers and increasing your association with Winners. Do this, and the odds will definitely turn in your favor!

CHAPTER 6
Intuitive Feelings— How To Take Advantage Of Them

The intuitive person is a lucky person. The good news is that *everyone* is intuitive, even those who insist that they do not believe in intuition.

Many people who fancy themselves to be "realists" do not believe in anything they cannot explain. They think intuition is some kind of metaphysical nonsense. Nothing could be farther from the truth. To discount the importance of intuition in attracting good luck and good fortune is to deny ourselves a golden opportunity to appraise the many chances that come to us in life.

Intuition, when properly understood, plays an important role in increasing our luck potential. It is a form of inner wisdom that communicates with us from the subconscious level of mind where all information and reference are stored.

Creative people rely heavily upon their intuitive perceptions. It is through intuition that gifted musicians, artists and writers have made contact with the Universal Mind, and then poured forth their inspiration to the world.

People considered to be of genius caliber are invariably those who have had the courage, confidence and daring to heed and follow the guidance of their own intuition. Such people do not really possess unusual powers. They are merely acknowledging what is inside us all. The difference is that they choose to *use* their intuition while others seem intent upon stifling it.

Do you think it might have been intuitive people that Henry David Thoreau was referring to when he wrote of those who respond to a "different drummer"? Not surprisingly, such people are often thought to be strange or eccentric. From childhood on, they are encouraged to be sensible, to adopt a more practical or realistic approach to life.

How much better it would be to take a more practical, more realistic approach toward intuition. From this moment forward, I urge you to think of it as a "success instinct," a guidance system that is constantly striving to steer you in the right direction. In some cases, it knows its target, goal or answer, and the objective is to reach it or to accomplish it. In other instances, where the target or answer is not yet known, the objective is to discover or locate it. Whatever the situation, intuition plays a vital role, for it keeps you informed when it is on the correct course, and also warns you when things are beginning to go astray. In the first instance, the little voice inside you will urge you to "just keep doing what you are doing." In the latter case, it will nudge you from within with the subtle (or possibly *not* so subtle) suggestion that you are starting to "get off the track."

Intuition is a means through which a higher form of intelligence attempts to voluntarily communicate with us. *It is always trying to do this*! We need not make any demands upon it, nor do we need to exert any effort to call it forth. It is there, just waiting to be heard!

THE ACCIDENT THAT DIDN'T HAPPEN

Any potential emergency which arouses the emotions and causes the heart to beat more rapidly, generally brings intuition into action. If you have ever experienced a close call, you may have felt that something came to your aid at the very last moment, and by split seconds, enabled you to avoid a serious accident. I think it would be safe to say that most of us have had such an experience. But not everyone gives credit to intuition in quite the same way that a close friend of mine does. She believes in intuition to such a degree that it is both an exciting and amusing experience to hear her talk about it.

One day, this friend started across the street when the Walk light came on, then suddenly stepped back up on the curb. Overpowered by a sudden impulse *not* to proceed, she had barely had time to reflect upon her actions when a car went flying past her at a speed in excess of a hundred miles per hour. The next morning, she read an article in the paper about a bank robber who was apprehended after a high-speed chase. Had my friend been in the crosswalk at the time this person drove by, she would have been instantly killed. As it was, she was alive and well, and more than a little eager to tell me about it.

The part I found so amusing concerned itself with her insistence that what she had actually been involved in was an "accident that didn't happen." Later, as I got to thinking about it, I decided she was right. All the elements of an accident were certainly present. A speeding car. A driver out of control. A potential victim. It was only my friend's intuition that altered the final outcome.

Admittedly, some people are more intuitive than others. This is because the frequency of intuition is known to vary greatly from one individual to the next. People who function more from their left brain or logical mind are generally less intuitive than those who function primarily through the right brain or creative thinking part of the mind. It is also believed that women are more intuitive than men, possibly because women have a predisposition to right-brain thinking, which is more in touch with their true feelings.

Intuitive people as a whole tend to be more self-confident and independent. Because of their healthy self-esteem, they are more inclined to open themselves up to unconventional ideas and messages that come from within. On the other hand, those who have an excessive need for security, who fear change and who cannot tolerate uncertainty, are also those who will close off the messages that were meant to assist them in taking advantage of luck-producing opportunities. Instead of being open to new ideas, such people seek to control every situation, to make their lives more predictable, and in the process, live under a rigid standard of rules that leaves no room for exploration, spontaneity or chance. Such people can often be heard to say: "It's impossible." "I just can't do it." "I'll never find the answer!" What they are actually doing is sending messages to their intuitive mind—telling it *not to bother*! But individuals with high self-esteem and self-confidence live with the conviction that they deserve and expect an answer to any situation or opportunity that confronts them. This, in itself, will stir their intuition to take positive action.

Make no mistake about it! Our luck-producing intuition can be increased proportionately to our attitude adjustment. It all goes back to the basic ways in which we feel about ourselves. If this is an area that needs attention in your life, you might wish to read two of my earlier books that deal with this subject: *The Ultimate Secrets of Total Self-Confidence* and *The Advanced Formula for Success*. Both will help you to achieve these goals in an easy, stress-free manner.

HUNCH VS. INTUITION

Somewhere in the cell structure of the brain there exists an organ which receives vibrations that are most commonly referred to as "hunches." Such knowledge is generally received when the mind is under the influence of heightened stimulation and should never be lightly dismissed. To call such knowledge a "hunch" is to underestimate its true significance.

To speak of hunches is to speak of a form of self-deception which comes from confusion between true intuition, conscious wishes and superstitions. The problem is that hunches invariably invite bad luck by causing us to underestimate the true risks in any situation. A hunch can make us overconfident and cause us to take reckless actions that are destined to bring us bad luck and misfortune.

From a prosperity standpoint, people have not always known what to do with their incredible powers of intuition. For the most part, they do not even understand what it is.

The word itself is derived from the Latin *intueri* which means "to see within, to consider, to contemplate." While philosophers and psychologists all have their own definitions of intuition, they basically agree with Webster's definition: *the act or faculty of knowing directly without the use of rational process*. Both philosophers and psychologists now recognize intuition as a natural mental faculty, a key element in generating creative ideas, forecasting the future and revealing inner truths.

Intuition comes on its own. You can no more force intuition than you can force someone to fall in love with you. In speaking of his own highly inspired works, Mozart once said, "Whence and how they come, I know not, nor can I force them." In other words, we can open our minds to intuition, and prepare ourselves for it by creating a mental and emotional environment in which it can properly thrive, but we cannot will it to occur upon demand. Nor should people make the mistake of believing that they can become more intuitive through positive thinking, through artificial enthusiasm, through autosuggestion, or some form of religious invocation.

You cannot fool the mind! It is done unto you as you believe—subjectively speaking. Your mind knows what you *really* believe and will only respond on that level. Whatever you might choose to believe intellectually will never override your self-doubts on an emotional level. The impact of your emotions will always be stronger!

GIVE INTUITION A CHANCE

Perhaps you have not followed your intuition because its urgings have often seemed so incredibly fantastic that it seemed best not to act. This is often the case with people who have reached some crisis point in their lives and who sense that they must now make some drastic changes if they hope to survive. Still, old habits die hard. Knowing that your health is being jeopardized by a high-pressure job that is netting you a six-figure income will not necessarily cause you to walk off calmly into the sunset. Although your health is being destroyed—although you may even die—there is still the matter of how you have always *lived*! Should you choose to reject your immediate lifestyle, it could well mean that you have been wrong! Wrong about the way you've been living—and thinking. No one likes to be wrong. Strange as it may seem, people would rather be right than happy. Still, that small inner voice refuses to go away. Despite your inner confusion and discomfort, it continues to urge you to take another path. What should you do?

First, let me tell you what *most* people would do. They would either ignore their intuition, or wait until they were able to reason through its promptings. But intuition is not *concerned* with reason. It is a faculty of the mind that does not explain. It simply points the way. After that, you are on your own to do or NOT do whatever you see fit.

Highly gifted people, and those who are thought to be incredibly lucky, are those who have enough self-confidence and faith in their intuition to see it through. Ordinary people, on the other hand, wait for "proof," and so, continue to flounder in the conflicts created by their own intellectual reasoning.

Before you can comfortably follow any intuitive path, it is necessary to understand that intuition is basically concerned with pointing the way to your greater good. That is its primary function and motive. *It wants what is best for you.* Always! Once you are able to accept this, you will automatically become more receptive to what it is trying to tell you, and after that, you will begin to notice some subtle changes taking place. For one thing, you will realize that intuition is actually right for you, that it is interested in you, that it knows all about you, and is determined to show you the proper way.

Where is the "proof" of this? Why, in your own faith that this incredible power exists! Notice how it gives you a greater ability to achieve, how it enables you to attract better conditions and happier experiences. The more you think about this kind and loving power, the more you will find intuitive guidance working with you and *for* you—and the easier it will become to accomplish your goals.

You will find this to be true in every area of your life, not only when it is necessary to make major life-altering decisions, but also when you suddenly need to "think on your feet."

Remember the friend I spoke of who had involved herself in an "accident that didn't happen"? As I've already told you, she is a great believer in intuition and constantly heeds its wise counsel in matters both great and small.

Early in her marriage, before she learned how to cook all the wonderful gourmet meals she regularly prepares today, she was faced with an unexpected and potentially catastrophic dilemma.

"My husband was a sales manager," she told me. "Occasionally, he would invite his sales crew out to dinner, but once, he invited the men, and also their wives, to have dinner with us in our home. Although I gave no outward indication, I was immediately thrown into a panic, for I barely knew how to boil an egg! In those days, I relied heavily upon convenience foods and frozen entrées to get me through the day. Now, suddenly, I was faced with the task of preparing a dinner for fourteen people, something I felt would need to be truly original, innovative and unique in order to engender pleasant memories long after the evening had passed.

"At the outset, the situation seemed impossible! I had no culinary skills—and yet, I wished to impress my husband, as all young brides are eager to do. The real question, of course, was *what* to do! As I silently stewed and fretted about it, the answer suddenly came! *If you can't be good, be a little outrageous. In the process, you might even be able to pass off your limited menu as a deliberate theme.*

"I began to think in terms of 'opposites,' inspired perhaps by my great affection for the original Odd Couple, Felix Unger and Oscar Madison. It occurred to me that Felix and Oscar had succeeded on the basis of being an unlikely combination. And so it was that I came up with an unlikely combination of my own—a dinner consisting of hot dogs and champagne! With all the fixings. Served on sterling silver trays.

"It turned out to be an exceptional evening, an incredibly warm and comfortable experience for everyone involved. After it was over, I knew I would be eternally grateful to that small inner voice that had guided me. The one that is guiding me still."

Have you ever had such an experience? Many people have. Just as many have received intuitive messages that proved to be essential to their safety or well-being. Just in the nick of time. Or so it seems.

The fact is, the source we have come to rely upon in unexpected situations is always there—and always stands ready to work for us.

Trust it.

Believe in it.

Start using it!

TRAINING YOURSELF TO "TUNE IN"

Intuition is similar to a radio receiver through which ideas, plans or thoughts flash into the conscious mind. Because our attention is most often tuned in to the outer world, we do not always hear or heed the guidance of intuition. Yet, if we were to keep a deliberate record of these intuitive promptings, we would be truly astonished at how often they actually speak to us.

How do they speak to us? And exactly what do they say?

It is important to understand that there are both *Yes* and *No* phases to intuition. Since the *No* phase may be a bit more predominant, it is often the only one that is really heard.

When intuitive messages in the *No* phase are ignored, their recipient will generally live to "rue the day."

"A little voice kept telling me not to do it! I should have listened. NOT listening was the worst mistake I ever made in my life!"

Because *No* messages tend to be louder and more emphatic, many people assume that this is the only way in which intuition even works. For one reason or another, it is always telling us NOT to do something. Nothing could be further from the truth! It is just that the *Yes* phase tends to work in quieter, more subtle ways, perhaps because it is less often concerned with critical situations and *more* often concerned with truly opportunistic ones.

You can most effectively contact the *Yes* and *No* phases of intuition by allowing yourself a period of solitude during the day—a time for quiet thought or meditation. Since intuition is not inclined to force its way into your conscious mind, it is important to create an atmosphere that is most conducive to its subtle yet powerful message.

As you begin to open yourself up to this wise Invisible Counselor, do not struggle, even in your thinking, to make things right or better. Instead, simply accept that whatever you think about, turn your attention to, or express any interest in, will gradually reveal its secrets to you. Before long, you will come to understand that the very thing you are concentrating upon *desires to know YOU!*

At this point, you will stop thinking of whatever it is you want or need as something separate and apart from yourself. You will stop thinking that it is difficult or even impossible to obtain. You will stop scheming, maneuvering and manipulating in order to gain your way. Instead, you will begin to realize that all things are already at hand, ready to present themselves to you in the form of new and exciting methods, ideas and plans.

At this stage, you will find that you have developed heightened abilities, and that you are also being instructed *from within* on many things you need to know. You will be delighted to discover that your incredible intuition, the very thing that has been prompting you, has already gone before, and prepared a way for you to follow. The strength and urgency of your desires is *proof-positive* that a way has already been prepared.

Now then, get ready for some surprises! Once you begin to trust your intuitive feelings, much good will come to you quickly, and without a struggle. Long-range goals will be realized much sooner than expected. At times, you will feel as if you are literally being showered with personal prosperity and good fortune.

Welcome to that select group of privileged individuals who always seem to be in the right place at the right time! The lucky ones! The Winners! Welcome to that happy and prosperous group who have developed an intuitive sense of what to choose, and when and how to act.

No longer will you be blocking off that natural flow of inner wisdom and knowledge. Nor will you see only negative messages in adverse circumstances, as you were once inclined to do.

Many years ago, Epictetus, the Greek philosopher, advised, "Whenever any chance befalls you, remember to ask yourself how you can put it to use."

The so-called "lucky" person is one who *expects* to be lucky, who permits his imagination to dwell in the positive realm rather than in the negative, and who is confident that he can respond to the opportunities of chance whenever they occur. This state of mind will quickly reveal the potential in every situation—yes, in *every* situation, not just in a few.

The basic idea behind the creation of good luck is this: *You cannot be lucky in life until you are lucky in your mind.* Mind is the creator of all that exists in the physical world. In the course of dealing with this incredible power that is Mind, it is important to sharpen every mental tool at your disposal. Intuition is one of those tools. Rather than making you lucky, intuition will assist you in *attracting* good luck, even as it points out the best direction for you to take. Conscious human reasoning is one thing, but never, never underestimate the potent sensitivity and power of intuition!

BECOMING A BETTER JUDGE OF CHARACTER

Intuitive feelings are very useful when dealing with others, providing as they do a quick estimate or "rundown" of a person's basic character and intentions.

On a nonintuitive basis, we are limited to judging a stranger by his appearance and superficial behavior. These are seldom if ever reliable. The intuitive person is more likely to have a "feeling" than an opinion on whether to trust or distrust, to like or dislike, to approve or disapprove of someone he must deal with. These unconscious impressions arise out of previous experiences with personality types who have demonstrated similar characteristics.

Just as there are people who can help us increase our good luck and good fortune, there are also those who will try to hurt us, or at the very least, bring out the worst in us.

I have always had a highly developed intuitive nature, and it often confused me because I did not always understand it. As a child, I could not really explain what it was that compelled me to like certain individuals, while distrusting and openly avoiding a number of others. In many cases, I was thought to be a snob but, more often than not, I was also right. Today, it is generally accepted that both children and animals have an extraordinary sense about certain things, and their own degree of receptivity is thought to provide a valuable gauge in judging strangers.

If children are more perceptive in an intuitive sense, it is only because they are using a God-given gift in an open, spontaneous way. Of course, this will quickly come to an end if adults continue to insist that they are behaving in a strange or abnormal way. All too often, parents, relatives and well-meaning friends will admonish children for not being more logical in their thinking.

"Grow up—get real—stop daydreaming!" are words a child frequently hears and eventually learn to obey. In the process, much is lost which must then be *relearned* later in life. So it is with intuition.

It is indeed fortunate that in this enlightened age, we are finally beginning to acknowledge certain powers of the mind that have long been neglected. Ironically, it is these unexplored faculties of the mind that seem to have the greatest power for producing a prosperous and successful life. Can you afford to ignore them? Hardly—for that would be equivalent to ignoring a major part of yourself.

All that you see in this world came about because of someone's inner vision, "feeling" or "intuition" that it could be done. Refusing to be impeded by those who thought them eccentric or abnormal, the great minds went on, thinking . . . constructing . . . inventing. Aren't you glad that they did?

And what about you? Can you afford NOT to follow the intuitive path, thereby suppressing those glorious dreams, those fantastic ideas and incredible feelings that persist in telling you that you were placed on this earth not only to BE, but to BE a WINNER? *Listen to that voice!* Allow it to communicate with you both in inner and outer ways.

In the former case, your intuition will speak to you through inner promptings, or in direct knowledge from within. But it may also speak to you through the words of a friend, through a phrase in a book or newspaper, or even through a series of events that take place around you.

Remain alert!

Observe—listen—and LEARN so that you can take advantage and profit from your intuition.

TESTING YOUR OWN INTUITION

How often does intuition enter into your life? How well do you avail yourself of it? Read the following questions and then mark the answers that you feel most accurately describe you:

1. Before attempting to solve any problem, I
   a) try to consider everything that is relevant to the issue.
   b) work my way systematically through every conceivable solution.
   c) play around with various ideas until something strikes my fancy.
2. When someone complains that they are not feeling well, I
   a) often know what is wrong.
   b) feel able to make a fairly accurate diagnosis after listening to the symptoms.
   c) feel totally in the dark on such matters.
3. Do you feel you have a kind of "instinct" for knowing when people are having personal problems?
   a) Yes.
   b) No.
   c) Only with those who are extremely close to me.
4. Would you say that all major decisions in your life have been based on logic?
   a) To some extent.

b) Yes.

c) No, I tend to trust my feelings.

5. If someone asks for your help in making a decision, how would you react?

   a) Try to find out what sort of an answer this person is seeking before actually suggesting anything.

   b) Base my answer on what my own feelings tell me would be right for him.

   c) Bring logical analysis to bear on the various options available.

6. Is it hard for you to do what you want when others attempt to discourage you?

   a) No. I am more inclined to follow my own feelings in the matter.

   b) Yes. When other people interfere, I tend to become confused.

   c) I am often influenced by the judgment of others.

7. If you dreamed that someone close to you had died, would you

   a) contact that person immediately?

   b) feel a bit disturbed, but think it would be silly to act on it?

   c) ignore it as a bad dream?

8. How do you tend to judge people when you first meet them?

   a) On the basis of personal appearance.

   b) By the things they say.

   c) By my own feelings about them.

9. Do you trust anyone else's intuition?

   a) Yes.

   b) No.

   c) At times.

10. Can you always be sure when people are telling you the truth?

   a) Always.

   b) Sometimes.

   c) Not usually.

11. Do you find that you tend to be thinking about someone just before he or she unexpectedly gets in touch with you?

   a) No.

      b) Sometimes.

      c) Often.

12. Do you think "women's intuition" is
      a) a polite term for a lack of logic?
      b) a reality?
      c) a myth?

ANALYSIS

Since the value of each most *intuitive* answer is 5, a perfect score would be 60. The lower your score, the less you are inclined to rely upon intuition.

Answers: 1) c 2) a 3) a 4) c 5) b 6) a
             7) a 8) c 9) a 10) a 11) c 12) b

5–15 score suggests you are an ultraconcrete thinker. It indicates you lack intuition more or less totally. It would seem that you don't want to admit that it could exist. Your tendency for concrete thinking limits you to stick to rigid, almost unimaginative solutions to almost every problem.

20–25 score suggests that you are a concrete thinker and have a basic distrust of intuition and a strong tendency toward concrete, hardheaded thinking. On the other hand, your resistance to your intuitive feelings may have something to do with accepting something you cannot fully understand or rationalize.

30–35 score suggests you are a semi-intuitive type who is skeptical about the value of intuition. However, unlike the first two types you are open to relying on your intuition on certain occasions while still not fully trusting it.

40–60 score suggests you are the intuitive type. You believe in intuition and are very intuitive yourself. Furthermore, your intuitive insights often pay off, saving you time while giving you the reputation of being a quick and purposeful thinker. This is a highly positive trait, however, you must remember to balance it with sound judgment so that you do not become overconfident or unrealistic. As with everything, BALANCE is the key word. Concrete thinking balanced with intuitive feelings will enable you to take advantage of your cognitive reasoning ability while enhancing it with your intuitive insights. This dynamic combination will allow you to take full advantage of your intuitive feelings and achieve results few people experience.

CHAPTER 7
How Winners Think Rich and Get Rich

Man was born to be rich, or grows rich by the use of his faculties, by the unison of thought with nature. Property is an intellectual production. The game requires coolness, right reasoning, promptness, and patience in the players.

—EMERSON

It's true! As a Winner, you deserve to be rich. One of your primary goals should be financial satisfaction and independence. Financial satisfaction enables you to enjoy what money you already have, even as you strive for financial independence.

Being financially independent means doing what you want to do, when you want to do it. I am so totally committed to this idea that I recently wrote an entire book around it. In case you have not read *Doing What You Love—Loving What You do*, its essence is simply this: The only way in which you will ever be financially satisfied and independent is to undertake some activity you love to do, and to incorporate it into your life's work.

The richest people in the world are those who thoroughly enjoy their career choices. "If I weren't being paid to do this," they insist, "I would still do it as a hobby." Can you say this about your present job or career? If not, then financial success will elude you until you find something you love to do and incorporate it into your life's work.

Another trait I have found that Winners share is that they focus on ideas that have a potential for *profit*. For some people, profit is a dirty word. However, before you can become rich, you must resign yourself to the fact that without a profit, there is no possibility of financial success.

Consider profit as a *reward* or financial *benefit* for serving others. The more you serve others, the more *profit* you can expect. And, you can only expect what you feel you *deserve*!

LACK CREATES LACK— MORE CREATES MORE

Whatever you focus your attention upon, you will tend to attract more of. If you focus on how little you have, that belief will soon become reinforced. A state of never-ending poverty is generally the result of intellectually and emotionally reinforcing poverty beliefs.

Do you feel you are afflicted with poverty beliefs? It is easy enough to find out. Simply ask yourself the three following questions:

1. Do I WANT to be rich?
2. Do I DESERVE to be rich?
3. Do I BELIEVE I can be rich?

The first question is one that most people would eagerly answer in the affirmative. Do they WANT to be rich? Yes! Yes! Yes! Beyond that point, however, it is common for negative thoughts to start creeping in.

A rather surprising fact of life is that so many people do not really feel that they DESERVE to be rich. They may not even KNOW this if they tend to feel undeserving on a purely subconscious level. As you might expect, this is generally the case. The reason for this is that many such feelings are often deep-rooted, and extremely difficult to dislodge.

Consider the outlook of a person who follows blindly in the footsteps of his father. "I'm just a coal miner," he may say. "My daddy was a coal miner before me, and his daddy before him. That's what we are. Coal miners."

Although coal miners certainly play a vital role in this country's industrial progress, it is the wrong profession for anyone who adopts it for the wrong reason. What your father or grandfather did for a living does not necessarily have anything to do with you.

People who do not believe they deserve to be rich are generally plagued with such hang-ups. If you have somehow managed to avoid the trap of doing whatever it is your father does, let me ask you this. Are you inclined to place certain negative connotations on money? Do you consider it the root of all evil? Do you feel it has a corruptive influence, that it destroys happiness, or increases your chances of coming to some "sorry end"? If you believe this, you are not alone. Many people feel the same. Such thoughts are a very real part of their Poverty Life-Script, which they are determined to play out. In other words, they are determined to lose.

Losing can be accomplished on a very subtle level—by involving oneself in bad investments, or by making loans to unreliable people who are not inclined to honor their debts. The possibilities are endless.

As concerns the last question—"Do I BELIEVE I can be rich?"— if asked to be totally honest, most people would be inclined to say, "No."

Our belief that we cannot become rich has its roots in the Judeo-Christian Work Ethic, which most of us have been exposed to since childhood. The Judeo-Christian Work Ethic implies that unless we *work hard* to earn our money, we are violating some kind of unwritten religious law. Of course, no such law even exists!

Having adopted the role of "hard-working stiff," we quickly become resigned to it, and afterward, console ourselves in odd ways. How often have you heard people make the following statements:

"Rich people are usually unhappy."
"If I ever came into a fortune, I'd immediately lose all my friends."
"Once you have a lot of money, you start to have a lot of problems."
"The people who have the big bucks usually made them dishonestly."

People who say such things may not really believe what they are saying, but it helps them to justify their losing status.

FIND THE MAGIC COMBINATION

Every contrivance known to man, every tool, instrument, article of furniture, every article designed for a specific use, originally evolved from some very simple beginning—and in its earliest stages, included some form of experimentation. We tend to experiment whenever we want to create something new, or improve anything that already exists.

How about you? Admittedly, you already exist, but if that is all you are doing, you may feel the need to do something bigger and better with your life. If so, good for you!

Ideas are the seeds of riches. And since there is no shortage of ideas, there can be no shortage of riches. If you are presently experiencing financial difficulties, it is because *you have not yet committed yourself to an idea that will reward you financially*.

Whatever the problem, you may be sure the solution already exists in one form or another. It may exist partly in what you are presently doing, or in some skill you have not yet taken the time to fully develop or refine.

Finding the right combination means taking a little of what you are doing, adding a little of something else, modifying it with things that others may have told you, subtracting whatever is counterproductive, and then arriving at a new combination—a *winning combination* that will enable you to unlock the door to success.

It is unfortunate that so many people disregard as *unreal* anything that is purely ideal and mental in nature, since that is where everything begins!

Spinoza once said, "A thing has only so much reality as it possesses power."

Yes, ideas have *power* and, given free rein, will help to bring you all that you desire.

MONEY IS AN IDEA IN ACTION

Even as you read these words, you have within you valuable ideas to improve your job, your business and community. Such ideas are deserving of your attention. They should be nurtured and encouraged to grow.

Ask yourself: *Where can I get help in actualizing my idea?* Start researching, then take it step-by-step. This is how all great fortunes are made.

As much as society struggles for economic equality, it will never be achieved. All social schemes intended to equalize the rich and the poor are doomed to failure. Since the beginning of recorded history, the rich have demonstrated a talent for becoming richer, while the poor have a tendency to stay poor. While this may not seem fair, the fact remains that the human mind is a creator as well as a destroyer. Whatever ideas we hold to be true must inevitably become our reality. The majority of the poor, in the course of continually programming their minds with poverty messages, insure that poverty will always be part of their lives. The only way they will ever escape poverty is to rewrite their Poverty Life-Script, replacing it with new ideas and beliefs that nourish their creative potential.

LIVING A CLICHÉ

Are you presently living your life in accordance with some familiar "catchphrase" you have been listening to since childhood? If so, you are living a cliché.

"Money doesn't grow on trees."
"Save your money for a rainy day."
"A penny saved is a penny earned."
"If you've ever been really poor, you can never be rich."

(NOTE: This particular cliché is a favorite of those who survived the Great Depression. The only problem is, they have not yet *survived* it—they are still experiencing it.)

Most of these counterproductive one-liners were passed down to us by our parents, who learned them from *their* parents, who learned them from *their* parents, who learned them—well, you get the idea. It is important to remember that a wrong concept can never become *right* simply through repetition. It can, however, gain a certain amount of credibility, which is extremely unfortunate for those who are easily influenced.

When you were a child, were you urged to think about the future in terms of achieving some measure of security?

> *"You're not getting any younger, you know. You've got to save for your old age."*
> *"What if your health fails?"*
> *"What are you doing to counter inflation?"*

What indeed! Although you can continue to badger yourself with a lot of anxious questions, it would be far better to face the truth about financial security. The truth is—*there is no such thing*! The only security you and I have is the ability to actualize, to make things happen through our own ideas and thoughts. If you manage to become proficient at this, you will always be in a position to replace what is lost. Bear in mind that no matter how much money you have, you could lose it at any moment. Millionaires have been known to go broke overnight. The ones who are able to recoup their losses are those who have learned the difference between being poor and being broke. They will be the first to tell you that being broke is a temporary situation, but being poor is a permanent state of mind.

REWARD IN PROPORTION TO RISK

As a professional handicapper, I have learned a lot about money management and odds. The bigger the risk, the greater the reward.

At the outset, it would be better to forget whatever you have ever been told about risk. We are not speaking of "plunging blindly" now, but rather of carefully calculating the odds and determining the real chances for success.

Do you think if you devoted yourself thoroughly to researching a particular subject, that you would eventually become an expert in that field? Would you say that the odds are in your favor? Of course they are! Unfortunately, most people would rather remain poor and ignore their true potential than to take a chance at excelling. They worry about failure, and loss.

"What if I LOSE everything?" they ask.

If you have ever asked yourself this question, bear in mind that you once had nothing and somehow managed to get where you now are. As concerns risk, if money is lost, you still retain the knowledge of how to earn it. No one can ever take THAT away from you!

In the end, the choice comes down to this: Would you rather be safe or rich? If you can't quite decide, I would urge you to think ahead.

WHAT IS THE WORST THAT CAN POSSIBLY HAPPEN?

Once you are able to face this question squarely, and to come to terms with it, you will be free to take risks.

Think about all the bad things that have ever happened to you. Which experience was the worst? What was the blackest day of your life?

What happened?

What happened next?

What happened after that?

Did you die? Obviously not. Were you financially ruined forever? Were you left without hope, with no means of ever recuperating from this devastating experience?

For the most part, people consider the most difficult times to be those when some *major changes* take place. In retrospect, they will generally admit that something good came out of it, that they are actually wiser and stronger for the experience.

How very fortunate it is that some Higher Power knows what it is we need to learn, since if it were left to us, we would never choose the harder road, the one that tests us and challenges us. And yet, that is what we need! To live in constant comfort is to stop growing. Nothing is required to maintain the status quo. And nothing of any real worth ever comes easy!

GETTING RICH QUICK

The appeal of getting rich quick is almost universal. In this Age of Instant Everything, we have become programmed for immediate gratification. Buy it now! Take it home today! No money down! No payments till next September!

People who have come to reject the idea of paying a price for success are frequently taken in by get-rich-quick schemes. They will invest in pyramid plans, in so-called once-in-a-lifetime opportunities, and of course, they are hopelessly addicted to the lottery.

Lotteries are one of the biggest scams operating today. They were designed to appeal to those who fantasize about becoming rich in a hurry. The lure of millions of dollars, the idea of instant wealth is a mesmerizing concept to those who have never learned how to channel their creative energies in the proper way. Such people hope to "fall into" the fortune they have never taken the time to *learn* how to *earn*.

Lotteries are non-positive expectancy games of chance. The odds of winning can be as high as 25 million to one. If you are determined to involve yourself in a game of chance, choose one that contains a positive expectancy factor, one that requires a certain degree of skill, and one that offers a positive return on your investment, providing the odds are in your favor.

As far as getting rich quick is concerned—forget it! It's a sucker's game.

HOW REALLY TO MAKE A MILLION

Yes, it is possible to make a million. Really! And realistically.

Consider this. If you were able to sell a thousand items at a net profit of a thousand dollars each, you would have one million dollars! When you think of it in that light, one million dollars isn't quite so mind-boggling, is it? In all the world, there must be a market of a thousand people who are willing and able to pay a thousand dollars for a specific product or service. The truth is, people are doing it all the time.

There is an important lesson to be learned from breaking down your goal into "manageable" pieces. In case you hadn't already guessed, it makes it much easier to achieve.

Early in my professional career, if I had pondered the thought of writing all the books that I presently have on the market, I would probably never have undertaken the task. The thought of writing even *one* book is intimidating enough, particularly on those days when it is difficult to find the right words. Rather than thinking about writing a book, I have always thought in terms of writing a certain number of pages per day. By faithfully adhering to this schedule, I eventually *end up* with a book. I can't help it!

If you would like to make a million dollars, rest assured that this is not an impossible goal. Others have done it, and so can you! Approach the challenge one stage at a time. It isn't necessary to acquire the entire amount in a single day. The important thing is to acquire it.

Take the first step.

Then the next.

Then the next.

Remember! Victory is not only a matter of achieving your goal. You are victorious for as long as you continue to work *toward* it!

Consider the alternative—a life of failure and poverty. A life of unrealized potential and limited thinking.

On the positive side, achieving your goal is easier than you think because you have so little competition! By that I mean that so few people are willing to pay the price for having what they want. Unfortunately, or perhaps fortunately for you, our society has fostered an "entitlement mentality." I have noticed this to be particularly true with teenagers and young adults. Many seem to believe that they are "entitled" to the benefits of hard work without paying the price. They have adopted the attitude that their parents or society "owe" them happiness and success just for being born.

I think the best illustration of this nonproductive entitlement mentality that I have ever seen is demonstrated in a satiric letter I came across from an unknown author who wrote about a comical little character which he or she called Homer Sneed.

In reaction to a government program that pays farmers not to raise already overabundant crops, Homer decides that the best way for him to achieve wealth is to go along with the system and to be paid for NOT doing something. In keeping with this non-productivity philosophy of life, Homer is prepared to make the following proposal to the United States Government:

U.S. DEPARTMENT OF AGRICULTURE
Gratuity Divison
Washington, D.C.

Gentlemen:

My friend over in Terreborne Parish received a $1,000 check from the government this year for not raising hogs, so I am going into the not-raising-hogs business next year.

What I want to know is, in your opinion, what is the best kind of farm not to raise hogs on and what is the best kind of hog not to raise? I would prefer not to raise Razorbacks but I would just as gladly not raise Berkshires.

The hardest part is going to be keeping an inventory of how many hogs I haven't raised. If I can get $1,000 for not raising 50 hogs, I will get $2,000 for not raising 100 hogs.

I plan to operate on a small scale right at first, holding myself down to about 4,000 hogs, which means I will have $80,000 coming from the government.

Now, another thing: these hogs which I will not be raising will not eat 100,000 bushels of corn. I understand that you also pay farmers for not raising corn. So, will you pay me anything for not raising 100,000 bushels of corn to not feed the hogs I am not raising?

I want to get started as soon as possible as this seems to be a good time of year for not raising hogs.

One thing more—can I raise 10 or 12 hogs on the side while I am in the not-raising-hogs business, just enough to get a few sides of bacon to eat??

Yours respectfully,
HOMER J. SNEED,
Farmer

While the anecdote of Homer Sneed is certainly an amusing extreme, it also deserves some serious thought. At least this character Homer Sneed realizes that, in order to survive, he must do *something*—in this case, "raise a few hogs on the side."

Unfortunately, most people who actually live by the something-for-nothing entitlement mentality are not even as smart as Homer

Sneed. They never fully realize that while waiting for their fantasy to come true, they had better "raise a few hogs on the side." Instead, they spend most of their lives waiting, wishing and hoping that someone will come along and take care of them and make their dreams come true. In the end, they die broke and disillusioned because life was "unfair." Society, or the imaginary people they were waiting for, didn't provide for them in the manner to which they felt they were entitled. This is a classic profile of a Loser.

Wouldn't you rather be a Winner? A Winner not only thinks rich but is willing to do whatever is neccessary to make it happen. If you are willing to think rich and pay the price to achieve the benefits of riches, here's the way to do it.

MASTER FORMULA FOR ACHIEVING RICHES

If you desire to be rich, you must think like a Winner. Winners have

1. Definite Ideas About How Much Money They Want
2. Persistent Desire to Be Rich
3. Confident Expectation of Financial Reward (Profit)
4. Unwavering Determination to Be Rich
5. Willingness to Pay the Price to Be Rich

I. DEFINITE IDEAS ABOUT HOW MUCH MONEY THEY WANT

Before you can achieve anything in life, you must know what you want. This is basic to any creative activity. Wanting "a lot of money" is insufficient information for your subconscious mind to process. Since "a lot" can be relative, your subconscious will not know how to direct you to your final goal. Start out by knowing *how much* you want. Be realistic. If ten thousand dollars seems like a lot of money to you, then start out with a lesser goal, something that's a little above your comfort zone but which you consider within the realm of human possibility. In other words, more than you are used to, but not something that seems totally impossible. After you have manifested that amount, you can gradually increase your goal.

2. PERSISTENT DESIRE TO BE RICH

Although you may want to be rich, you may not desire it enough. Many so-called desires are actually wishful thinking. You must have a burning desire. Remember, *desire is the seed of opportunity*. Whatever you do not desire strongly enough will elude you. Whatever you desire or feel most strongly about will be attracted to you.

3. CONFIDENT EXPECTATION OF FINANCIAL REWARD (PROFIT)

You must expect to be justly compensated for your ideas and efforts. Keep in mind that there is no reason to feel guilty when you earn a profit from taking risks and actualizing your money-making ideas.

4. UNWAVERING DETERMINATION TO BE RICH

Winners are determined to continue to advance in the face of every obstacle. They are not easily discouraged by occasional roadblocks. They do not allow themselves to be defeated by obstacles. To them, an obstacle is merely an opportunity in disguise. Some of their most successful money-making opportunities started out as obstacles.

5. WILLINGNESS TO PAY THE PRICE TO BE RICH

Winners are willing to pay their dues. They don't expect something for nothing. The price that Winners pay to be rich is to follow these five steps.

There you have it! The Master Formula for Achieving Riches. It you find you are weak in some areas, don't get down on yourself. Remember, you are growing and learning how to be rich. You have good reason to be proud of past accomplishments, and as a Winner, if you will THINK rich, you can BE rich!

SPECIAL BONUS
HOW YOU CAN BE A WINNER
WITH A MILLION DOLLARS

This is a special bonus for my young readers or parents with young children. I want to share an idea with you that will make you a WINNER WITH A MILLION DOLLARS by the time you are age sixty-five. It is so simple and so effective, you will probably wonder why you never considered it before.

The law of mathematics tells us that if we invested a given amount of money at 9 percent, we could double our money in eight years. How can this make us a million dollars? Let's work this backward.

If you wanted to accumulate a million dollars by age sixty-five you would need to put away the following amounts at 9 percent interest:

Age 57 $500,000
Age 49 $250,000
Age 41 $125,000
Age 33 $ 62,500
Age 25 $ 31,250

If you can put together $31,250 by the time you are twenty-five or $62,500 by the time you are thirty-three, you'll have enough saved at that time so that *you will never have to save another dime for the rest of your life*!

To put this in perspective, let's take the $31,250 figure. This is about a year of income for a college graduate with a few years of work experience. Take it back another eight years and the cost is $15,625—about the price of a shiny new automobile (Highly Depreciable Asset).

A million dollars may not be what it once was, but it is still a lot of money—far more than most people will accumulate in a working lifetime. Yet if looked at from the other end of a working career, the possibility of a million-dollar retirement is no more than a year of income or, maybe, that new car you could put off purchasing.

Early savings could produce some major lifetime benefits such as:

* Eliminate the need to save more, later, for longer
* Eliminate the worry about Social Security
* Eliminate the worry about corporate pensions
* Provide an above-average retirement income for as long as you live

Still nervous about getting the original sum together? That's understandable, so let's extend the deadline another eight years. If you can't put the money together by the age of twenty-five or thirty-three, you can still retire with a million if you manage to put together $125,000 by the time you are forty-one.

While this figure is less scary than $1 million, it is still far more than most people accumulate. So the question remains: How do you put the original stake together?

One possibility is a gift from a wealthy parent or grandparent. Putting away the necessary sum when you are young can do a great deal more than a much larger inheritance later. However, since most of us do not have wealthy relatives, we must consider a more practical alternative.

There is another way, one that doesn't require anything but the commitment to save a little every year: Set up an IRA (Independent Retirement Account). Whether the distribution is tax deductible or not, the annual earnings are tax deferred, and putting away $2,000 a year will accumulate the stake you need.

If for instance, you put aside $2,000 a year from age twenty-one to age forty-one and earn 9 percent compound interest, you will amass just over $120,000. If you save and are committed to your goal, it can be done quite easily. Remember, this is not a lifetime savings project. Just put aside $167.00 per month for somewhere between twelve and twenty years when you are young and you will have a cool million at sixty-five. That comes out to about $5.50 a day!

Easier said than done, of course. But consider trying to do the same thing from the other end of your working life. If you start saving at fifty (as most people do) you'll need to put aside about $26,000 per year to accumulate the same million by the time you are sixty-five. It may be difficult to give up $5.50 a day when you are in your twenties, but it is virtually impossible to save $2,000 a month when you are in your fifties.

Can you see the possibilities here? Ninety-five percent of the people in this country are financial Losers at age sixty-five. You don't have to be one of them. If you are a parent or a grandparent, you can help your offspring to achieve this worthy goal. If you are a young reader, I urge you to consider the above. It's easy to accomplish, it's practical, it will build your sense of self-discipline and self-confidence, and most of all, you will be able to say, "I am a Winner with a Million!" This is how Winners Think Rich and Get Rich!

CHAPTER 8
How The "Attitude Of Gratitude" Increases Your Win Factor

One of the key principles responsible for increasing your Win Factor concerns itself with giving or "outflowing." The universe consists of pure energy, and this energy is in a state of constant flux. Once you fully understand the nature of this inflow and outflow, you will find it possible to tune into its constant, steady rhythm. The main thing to remember is this: *In order to increase inflow, it is necessary to proportionately increase outflow.* As you give of your own energy and substance, you will automatically create a space for more to flow in.

Many people who have never acquired a "giving" nature have failed to do so out of fear. What they actually fear is that there will not be enough to go around. It is a ludicrous idea at best since the universe is a source of constant abundance. Everything we need is always available to us. Ample opportunities, a constant flow of money, never-ending ideas, wonderful dreams and all the right people and circumstances to assist us in making those dreams a reality. Do you doubt it? Then you are ignoring yet another area of abundance in your life, your own inner talents, experience and knowledge. While these are frequently ignored or underestimated, they are the most valuable assets you will ever possess!

LEARNING TO GO WITH THE FLOW

What we are basically concerned with here is the *outflow* rather than the inflow. Why? Because when you cling too tightly to what you have, you must inevitably lose it.

Look at those who are constantly lacking. Notice how tightly they grasp at life. Notice too how little they have, and how luck seems to constantly elude them.

"I'll never get ahead!" is a common complaint, and one that may well be true. I would urge you not to identify with such people since there is nothing to be gained by feeling wronged, or cheated, or "hexed." When you begin to believe such things, all you are doing is piling one negativity on top of another. Try to understand that it is your own desperation and despair that is cutting you off from a flow of good luck. It is because you are preoccupied with taking rather than giving that you feel limited and constantly in need.

AN ATTITUDE OF GRATITUDE

It is important to be grateful for whatever you have, no matter how little it may be. And, of course, you should never allow yourself to make comparisons, since if you persist in evaluating your own personal or monetary worth against another's, you are doomed to eternal discontent. There will always be some who have more, or who *seem* to have more, but what has that to do with you? When you have an attitude of gratitude, you are living with the positive affirmation that there is no real lack in your life. And once you freely acknowledge this, you will begin to activate the seed of abundance that must inevitably produce even *more*.

While this is a wonderful thing to know, it should never become your underlying motive for gratitude or giving. You should never think in terms of how much you will NEED to give, as if it were a price to be paid for something you desire in return. Gratitude and giving are ends in themselves. They enable us to grow in both mental and spiritual ways, opening our minds to the abundance of the universe, to its infinite wisdom, substance and power. It is only when we let go of our limited thinking that we can expand into a larger life where proper thoughts and proper actions will help to insure our prosperity.

BEING A GOOD RECEIVER

It isn't only football players that need to perfect this skill. The fact is, many givers are also bad receivers. An unwillingness to accept what others have to give is often perpetuated by the desire for control. There are those who through their own acts of generosity, seek to make others dependent upon them. And, of course, there is also the long-suffering or martyristic motive.

In your own life, I would urge you to strive for a healthy balance between giving and receiving, thereby enabling others to enjoy the same good feelings that *you* enjoy whenever you perform a kind or generous act.

INCREASING YOUR WIN FACTOR THROUGH GRATITUDE

Here are some highly effective ways in which to increase your Win Factor through an Attitude of Gratitude:

1. Take the time to express appreciation to others in as many ways as possible—through a letter or card, a phone call, a gift, a word, a touch.
2. Practice using more words of appreciation and thanks for whatever you have. Remind yourself often, and say these words aloud. Tell others how grateful you are for the abundance in your life, realizing even as you do so that you are effectively applying the principle of positive affirmation.
3. Practice telling others how grateful you are to *them* for what they have contributed to your life. "It was kind of you to help me." "I want you to know how much I appreciate you." "Thank you for the wonderful surprise."

4. Sort through your possessions and dispose of items you no longer need so that others may benefit from their use. Don't be afraid to let go! You can replace what is given away with newer and better things, but first, you must make way for something newer and better to come into your life.
5. Refuse to save money out of the fear of not having enough. This kind of fear is a self-fulfilling prophecy and, eventually, will cause you to lose what you have. Allow yourself an occasional extravagance, take a friend to dinner, contribute to a worthy cause. Every action of this kind is living proof that you have faith in universal abundance, and the law of inflow and outflow.
6. Give of your own energy. Share your ideas and creative talents with others. Help them succeed and your own success will multiply. Remember! To the extent that you demonstrate an Attitude of Gratitude, your Win Factor will proportionately increase.

GIVING—THE KEY TO A MORE EXPANSIVE LIFE

What you are trying to do while you live on this earth is to create a beautiful person. The law of giving will open up new horizons for you and broaden those you already have. It will expand your character and personality. It will place you in the company of those who have helped transform the world, and give new meaning to your life. Yes, giving can do that, and *should* do that, and *will* do that, if it is done in the proper way.

What do you give of yourself emotionally? Do you take pride in maintaining a stoic attitude during times of stress and despair? What do you think you are in danger of losing or destroying in the course of "revealing" yourself? Isn't it possible that others would gravitate toward you out of a sense of "having walked in your shoes"? Isn't it possible that something productive, something good, something character-building could come out of what you perceive to be an emotional weakness, out of your need to give away some aspect of yourself that you have always attempted to conceal?

You can literally starve yourself by withholding yourself from others, by refusing to enter into friendships, or loving relationships, since the law of abundance is also the law of privation. Yes, it IS a two-way street!

SCATTERING YOUR SHOT

Having talked about people who do not know how to give, let us now talk about people who do not know the *proper way* in which to give. Quite often, these are persons who give a miniscule amount of their money or time to a number of worthy causes. The problem is that they give so little of themselves or their resources that it hardly makes a difference. Here again, the object is to be *seen* as a giver, which may not really have anything to do with *wanting* to do good. Scattered giving can bring scattered, ineffectual results, both for the giver and the recipient. How much more effective it would be to concentrate on one major mission, to believe that you can make a monumental difference by devoting yourself with zealous dedication and determination to one incredible cause.

Do not concern yourself with what will happen to *you*—the giver. Do not depend upon persons or conditions for your prosperity. Simply allow the power and abundance of the universe to provide you with a constant source of supply. It will, you know, once you open the door and allow it to enter.

DEVELOPING AN ATTITUDE OF GRATITUDE

At times, the only way to develop an Attitude of Gratitude is to deliberately remind yourself of the many things you have to be grateful for. One way of doing this is to properly acknowledge yourself, and also, significant others in your life. If you are not accustomed to thinking along these lines, it may be difficult at first. A good way to get started is to make an actual list.

Can you think of *fifteen positive things* about yourself? Do the best you can, and when your list is completed, see if you can think of additional things to be added.

LIST OF PERSONAL ATTRIBUTES FOR WHICH I AM GRATEFUL

1.
2.
3.
4.
5.
6.
7.
8.
9.
10.
11.
12.
13.
14.
15.

If you found it difficult to think of fifteen positive things to say about yourself, do not despair. All it really means is that you have somehow gotten out of the habit of seeing yourself in a good light. Some possible answers might well have included the following:

1. Talented
2. Determined
3. Creative
4. Practical
5. Likable
6. Flexible
7. Enduring
8. Self-Assertive
9. Well-Organized
10. Versatile
11. Loyal

12. Loving
13. Honest
14. Level-Headed
15. Generous.

Although I do not know you personally, I am willing to bet that I've listed a lot of your own outstanding attributes, and possibly some you did not think to list yourself. Can you see how much you have to be grateful for? I sincerely hope you do! Now then, let's move on to the second list.

This time, I would like you to list all the significant others in your life, anyone who has encouraged you, inspired you and helped you to become the person you are today. Think hard and try to include everyone who has had some lasting influence upon your life, and those with whom you have shared some truly memorable experiences.

PEOPLE I AM TRULY GRATEFUL TO HAVE KNOWN

1.
2.
3.
4.
5.
6.
7.
8.
9.
10.
11.
12.
13.
14.
15.

You may have found this list somewhat easier to compile than the previous one, and perhaps some of the answers surprised you. Did you find yourself thinking of people you hadn't thought about in years? People who were once very near and very dear to you? Yes, we *do* tend to forget. We stop being grateful.

And now, on to the last list. This will be a list of personal achievements. While many may have faded from your mind, I urge you to recall them now. Go back as far as you can. No success, however small, should be considered insignificant.

MY LIST OF PERSONAL ACHIEVEMENTS

1.
2.
3.
4.
5.
6.
7.
8.
9.
10.
11.
12.
13.
14.
15.

In compiling this list, did you find yourself itemizing such accomplishments as the first gold star you ever earned in kindergarten? If so, good for you! When considered in its proper context, that gold star was as much of an accomplishment as anything else that you have ever done. The object then was to excel. And you did. Just as you are doing now.

On the off-chance that you may have had some trouble with this list, let me once again supply you with some hypothetical answers. See if you can relate to any of them and, if so, feel free to adopt them as your own.

MY LIST OF PERSONAL ACHIEVEMENTS

1. Local spelling bee champion—7th grade
2. High school homecoming queen
3. Class valedictorian
4. Starting my own business
5. My marriage
6. Motherhood
7. Consistent progress in my chosen field
8. A long friendship
9. Increased income
10. Sales contest winner
11. Weight loss
12. Painting my house
13. Improved relationships with coworkers
14. Learning a foreign language
15. Welcoming a newcomer
16. Winner of safe driver award
17. Successful fund-raiser
18. Planting a beautiful garden
19. Earning my college degree
20. Cooking a gourmet meal

In compiling a list of achievements, you will soon come to realize that you have had many successes in life—in other words, that you have much to be grateful for. Although this is obviously true, most people are more inclined to concentrate on anything that *doesn't* work out instead of all the things that *do*. Once you fall into this habit, it becomes easier to accept that "luck" is never with you. But now you can see that it is. In actuality, most things tend to work out and, because they do, we give them little attention. Perhaps you should take the time to do that right now.

Think back.

Remember.

Be grateful!

THE GREATEST GIFT OF ALL

The greatest gift of all costs us nothing. It is something we have to give regardless of our immediate financial condition. What we are talking about here is the gift of love and friendship. Every act of love and friendship toward others increases our own luck-potential. The key to genuine friendship and love exists in our desire to have others feel loved and accepted. In this case, we are not talking about a superficial attitude of friendliness, but rather genuine caring and concern for those with whom we come in daily contact.

Every act of true friendship and love sets certain forces into motion that have a positive influence upon our ability to attract more good luck and good fortune into our lives. *Such actions never go unrewarded.* Of course, the reverse is also true. Any *negative* actions toward another immediately cancel out the Law of Circulation and Good Luck.

LAW OF CIRCULATION AND GOOD LUCK

A clear understanding and wise use of this basic law will quickly enough determine the degree of our power to attract good luck and good fortune. Most unfortunate or unlucky people have failed (either consciously or unconsciously) to cooperate with the Law of Circulation, thereby producing negatively charged bad luck into their lives.

Exactly what IS the Law of Circulation? It is one that has been shared by every great teacher since the beginning of time. In essence, the Law of Circulation simply states "As you give, so shall you receive." The opposite of the Law of Circulation is, of course, selfishness and greed. NOTE: These reflections of spiritual weakness are *guaranteed* to attract only bad luck and misfortune with painful regularity.

REAPING THE RESULTS

It should be noted that positive actions do not necessarily bring immediate results. Think of it as making deposits in a Universal Bank. Eventually, your account will become quite large and you will be able to draw upon extremely generous reserves.

Another interesting fact to consider is that you will seldom receive back from the same people you give to. In other words, the people you are most generous toward are least likely to reciprocate, and your own inner disappointments generally stem from this totally unrealistic expectation.

How often have you been hurt because you did something for someone and they didn't seem to appreciate it, or didn't respond in kind? The real problem exists in your insistence that the Law of Circulation work through the people you give to. Occasionally, it will. More often, it won't. Still, it works!

On those occasions when I have made personal "loans" to people, I have told them not to pay the money back to me. I have asked instead that they pass it on to some other needy individual and instruct *that* person to do the same. This not only frees me from any unrealistic expectations, it also opens the door to other unknown and unexpected sources of return.

I prefer not to loan money to anyone unless it is a business transaction. In every other instance, I would rather *give* than *loan*. In my own mind, I have sent the loan out into the Law of Circulation, which will eventually come back to me in better ways than I could ever imagine.

From my personal point of view, the best possible return for any gift, material or otherwise, is in the sharing of an "idea." If I can receive one good idea that will change my personal or financial situation for the better, I consider myself paid-in-full with interest! The principles I have shared with you in this book have always enabled me to take any good idea and multiply it many times over in a positive and profitable way. And the same can hold true for you!

By cooperating with the Law of Circulation, you will open your awareness to new and beneficial ideas. You will also enhance the awareness of others around you as they witness your true, uncalculated generosity. Finally, the Law of Circulation will increase the probability that those others will contribute an idea or offer a solution that will prove beneficial to your own best interests, one that is sure to reward you handsomely for the rest of your life.

CASHING IN ON YOUR OWN MISTAKES

What is your Attitude of Gratitude toward making a mistake? Are you humbled or humiliated by the experience? Why not be grateful for it, for what it has actually taught you?

Lesson No. 1: In order to correct a mistake, you are automatically forced into a positive plan of action. First, you must acknowledge the error, then track it down and pinpoint its cause. In the process, you will learn to face the problem squarely, and to assume full responsibility for whatever now needs to be done.

Lesson No. 2: More often than not, some kind of action is called for after an error is made. The time to act is immediately! In this, there is another good lesson to be learned—namely, the need for overcoming the habit of procrastination.

Lesson No. 3: Many mistakes are made because of a lack of information or knowledge. Should this turn out to be the problem, then what you will learn is to better prepare yourself, to "bone up" where your knowledge is weak.

Lesson No. 4: Once you have learned to face up to a mistake, you can often take it a step further and actually conjure up a way to use it to your advantage. NOTE: *Every mistake should be examined with this possibility in mind.*

Lesson No. 5: Finally, you can learn from the mistakes made by others. It really isn't necessary to commit them all yourself!

Yes, mistakes are great teachers, and since that is true, you should always be grateful for what you can learn from them.

IN SUMMARY

Overall, gratitude is its own reward. The more you find to be grateful for, the better you will feel. And the better you feel, the more open you will be to that wonderful Win Factor in your life. Remember! It is always there, just waiting to be utilized in the proper way. Assuming you are now ready to accept this as a basic law of the universe, would you say you have a legitimate reason to feel "lucky" today? Good!

You may have heard the old saying "If you want to make it a better world, then start with yourself." Well, an excellent way to begin is with an Attitude of Gratitude.

It's guaranteed to make you a Winner!

CHAPTER 9
"Win Therapy"—
A Model Of Success

Throughout my life I have been fortunate to have several mentors. These were individuals who had mastered their area of expertise and were willing to share their knowledge with me. In some instances, I sought them out, and in other instances, they came into my life just when I needed them.

I believe that the concept of "modeling" is one of the most powerful secrets to achieving success. Essentially, modeling is seeking out an individual that has achieved outstanding success in the field in which you are involved, and then modeling yourself after their success.

It is not necessary to reinvent the wheel. I can assure you that whatever you want to achieve, there is someone, somewhere, who has already achieved the same goal. All you need do is find that person, study their success, and *do what they do*. These people are Winners! Unfortunately, most Losers model themselves after other Losers.

ATTRACTING A TEACHER

You have undoubtedly heard the saying *"When the student is ready, the teacher will appear."* What this really means is that when we are ready to accept something we truly desire, we will consciously and unconsciously attract the people, circumstances and conditions necessary to the fulfillment of that desire. It is the same principle that causes Winners to attract Winners and Losers to attract Losers.

While Losers may come in many varieties, the most common stereotypical image is that of the so-called "compulsive gambler." This is a person who goes to a casino or racetrack armed with little knowledge and a "lucky" feeling that invariably causes him to lose his shirt.

Once I had decided to take up thoroughbred handicapping as a hobby and a serious form of investment, I immediately found myself questioning whether or not I was doing the "right" thing. Like so many others, I had been programmed to believe that all gamblers eventually LOSE. Also, because of my religious background, I had been programmed to believe that gambling is basically "evil," and at the very least, not a socially acceptable means of earning money.

The word "gamble" in itself is loaded with morality injunctions, except in the case of those who "gamble" on stocks, bonds, commodities and real estate. Such people are not thought to be "gamblers" but "investors." No longer able to ignore the contradiction in this, I decided to reconsider the matter in a more realistic light.

I turned to Webster for a definition of terms. Here is what I found:

INVESTMENT: *"To lay out money or capital in BUSINESS with the view of obtaining an income or profit."*

GAMBLING: *"To PLAY or game for money or other stakes."*

It is easy to see that, by definition, the only distinction between these two words is that one is considered *work* and the other is considered *play*.

THE ROLE OF RELIGION

Since most of us have been influenced by the religious Judeo-Christian "work ethic," we are programmed to believe that only socially acceptable "work" occupations are "good." Thus, one who receives income from "investing" in stocks, bonds, commodities or real estate is felt to be "working" and, because of this, is termed an "investor."

The gambler, however, by arbitrary religious and moral definition, is "playing," which is in direct opposition to the moral teachings of the Judeo-Christian work ethic. Therefore, the gambler's activities must be "evil" or "bad." If he wins, his unearned winnings are considered an instrument of the Devil. If he loses, he is getting what he deserves.

In my own case, I was winning more than I was losing, which, for a time, concerned me deeply. Was I doing the Devil's work?

THE TEACHER APPEARS

At this point I was ready to meet my Teacher and, apparently, he was also ready for me! His name is Howard Sartin, Ph.D., a psychotherapist who specializes in the diagnosis and treatment of so-called "compulsive" or "pathological" gamblers. I first heard about him when I read an article about his unique approach to rehabilitating problem gamblers, which he called "Win Therapy."

I wrote to Dr. Sartin to ask him if he would mind sharing some of his ideas behind the concept of Win Therapy. By way of professional introduction, I enclosed a copy of one of my books. A week or so later, I received a package in the mail along with a nice note that read as follows: *"You are already quite popular around here. We keep your books in stock for our clients. In fact, I just purchased two dozen copies and only have six left."*

It's interesting, if you look at the whole picture. Here was a man I had never before met but was attracted to through reading a professional journal. By the same token, he had never met me and had no way of knowing that the author of the books he was recommending was also interested in professional handicapping. Coincidence? I think not!

I am sharing this with you because I think you will find Dr. Sartin's work, and the basis of his Win Therapy, both interesting and supportive of the ideas discussed in previous chapters.

Since 1975, Dr. Sartin has assumed an adversary role towards the American Psychiatric Association in the diagnostic philosophy and treatment practices for treating so-called "compulsive" or "pathological" gamblers. It is important to note that after twelve years of successful treatment, Dr. Sartin has proven that

the terms "compulsive" or "pathological" are a gross ~~~~
Rather, he has correctly diagnosed "compulsive" or "~~~~
gamblers as "Losing" gamblers, or L.G.'s.

His first experience with problem gamblers involv~~~~ ~~up
of truck drivers who had been convicted of gambling-r~~~~ated fe-
lonies and high misdemeanors. The court had granted them the
use of provisional driver's licenses so that they could continue to
earn a living *provided* they also entered into psychotherapy or
Gamblers Anonymous treatment programs.

Both Alcoholics Anonymous and Gamblers Anonymous base
their rehabilitative practices on the concept of total ABSTI-
NENCE. Although the members of this group had already been
exposed to Gamblers Anonymous, their urge to gamble had not
abated. If anything, they were becoming increasingly eager to
"try their luck" again.

Personality testing has shown that gamblers generally have a
higher-than-average IQ. This was proven out when this group
began to sense that there were certain fallacies in the ABSTI-
NENCE theory postulated by Gamblers Anonymous. Their sus-
picions were altogether correct. While many gamblers have joined
Gamblers Anonymous hoping to "cure" their problem, the actual
cure rate—successful abstinence—of Gamblers Anonymous is 3.5
percent. For other psychiatric treatment programs, the rate is
LESS than 3 percent.

Since the scandal of the great baseball player Pete Rose, *addiction* is the manifestation of problem gambling that most concerns society in general. What Dr. Sartin has shown through his
research and successful treatment procedures is that "compulsive" or "pathological" gamblers *are not addicted to gambling*.
Rather, they are addicted to LOSING.

His most significant discovery was that the gambler's true *pathology* is not gambling, but LOSING. This is characterized by a
gambler's inability to distinguish between *positive* and *nonposi-
tive* or *negative* expectancy events. Gamblers live in a fantasy
world wherein they continue to visualize the "big score" without
evaluating (through knowledge of the odds and probabilities)
their actual chances for success.

According to Dr. Sartin, THE CURE FOR LOSING IS . . . WIN-
NING! While, at first glance, this may appear overly simplistic,
it has nonetheless proven to be the most effective treatment available today for treating problem gamblers.

The fact is, few psychiatrists, psychologists or health care professionals are equipped to treat the problem gambler. Along with Gamblers Anonymous, they tend to recommend immediate and total abstinence. While abstinence is certainly essential in the early stages of treatment, it need not be maintained once the client/patient is "cured."

The "cure" lies not in abstaining from gambling, but rather in abstaining from any form of risk-taking that does not produce a positive expectancy. In this case, positive expectancy is defined as any form of investment that can be expected to produce a positive return if the odds are in the investor's favor.

The goal of Win Therapy is to turn "compulsive" or "pathological" gamblers, which Dr. Sartin prefers to call "Losing Gamblers" (L.G.'s) into "Winning Investors" (W.I.'s). The treatment program encompasses a twofold process which includes both psychological reprogramming and educational retraining. The educational aspect is concerned with the implementation of a methodical process for *winning*. This, of course, must be accompanied by a winning *belief system*. Both Dr. Sartin and I have repeatedly proven that unless a person fully *expects* to win, there is no way that he *will* win in the long run. His thought processes will lead him to failure. (Sound familiar?)

Dr. Sartin began to study all aspects of gambling to develop a winning methodology. After extensive research, he came to the conclusion that thoroughbred horse racing, combined with pari-mutuel wagering, was the *best* and *only* form of gambling that could be expected to produce a positive expectancy outcome.

Under the pari-mutuel system, after the racetrack takes a given percentage of the day's take, they return approximately 85 percent of the money taken in to the patrons. This is in direct contrast to casinos, which return less than 15 percent of the money wagered back to their patrons.

To further understand Dr. Sartin's reasoning for choosing pari-mutuel wagering as part of his treatment procedure, we need to take a look at some interesting statistics. Since the inception of pari-mutuel wagering, daily statistics have consistently shown that 80 percent of those who wager at pari-mutuel racetracks will lose money, 15 percent will break even, and only 5 percent will win.

At a major track such as Santa Anita, where the DAILY handle is apt to exceed $6 million, 85 percent of that is redistributed to the 5 percent winners. This means that 5 percent of the total patrons split up approximately $5,100,000! The distribution process itself works out like this:

60%   of the money goes to daily winners whose success is irregular and based on minimum skill.

25%   goes to winners who win with some degree of frequency through a combination of skill and random chance.

15%   goes to highly skilled handicappers who make comparable profits *consistently* throughout the year.

While the professional handicapper's profit is smaller, it is subject to only minor fluctuations and vagaries. The composition of the first two groups, however, changes daily.

Because the smaller group is more consistent, its annual earning potential based on forty weeks out of the year can be expected to exceed $85,000 per year. In addition, the average professional handicapper's R.O.I. (Return On Investment) per year consistently outperforms the best mutual funds on the market.

Armed with this information and a thorough background in clinical psychology, Dr. Sartin set out to develop his controversial Win Therapy program.

His first group of problem gamblers entered into a clinical contract requiring that no wagers would be placed until Dr. Sartin and his group could consistently produce a *minimum* win factor of 45 percent, at an average mutuel payoff of $8 on a $2 wager. This also included the use of a money management process that assured them of a profit.

They were also required to attend group-therapy sessions designed to reprogram their Losing life-script. Since handicapping is not the Losing Gambler's primary problem, Dr. Sartin placed most of the emphasis upon psychological retraining. He has repeatedly proven that a mediocre handicapper with a *winning* attitude will be more successful in the long run than an expert handicapper with a *losing* attitude.

Dr. Sartin is now retired from full-time practice, but the number of problem gamblers he has successfully treated attests to the success of his Win Therapy program. Since 1975, he has treated over eighteen hundred problem gamblers, most of whom were diagnosed by other mental health professionals as "compulsive" or "pathological" gamblers. Of that number, 17 percent proved to be true recidivists who could not be cured. Another 25 percent stopped gambling on their own after they had been effectively treated and had seen it demonstrated that pari-mutuel events could be won on a consistent basis. At this juncture, they no longer needed the emotional release of losing, or the pathological "thrill" that came from anticipating a "big score."

This left about 850 patients who vowed to give up all gambling except thoroughbred handicapping, which they now saw in terms of "investing" rather than "gambling." Once they were taught how to become pari-mutuel *investors*, they no longer lost money at gambling-related activities. In fact, their personal incomes increased dramatically.

At last count, 60 percent of them were making a substantial living at professional handicapping, 40 percent were making a part-time income and showing constant improvement. Overall, this amounts to an 83 percent *success rate*! It also proves that Losing Gamblers can be turned into *Winning Investors*!

Thoroughbred handicapping is not for everyone. However, from my own experience, I know that it can be a highly enjoyable and profitable hobby or profession. The secret of success in this field is acquiring expert knowledge in handicapping, as well as the necessary psychological training to become a consistent Winner. If you would like more information on this subject, I recommend that you contact Thoroughbred Research, Inc., 2961 Industrial Rd Suite 444, Las Vegas Nevada 89109

PUTTING IT ALL TOGETHER

The most significant part of the conversion from "Losing Gambler" to "Winning Investor" did not come from the handicapping methods alone. Its true essence lies within the psyche of the individual who learned to change his/her Loser self-image to that of a Winner.

Dr. Sartin's psychotherapy approach is patterned strongly upon Transactional Analysis, which was pioneered by Eric Berne, M.D., author of *Games People Play*. Because he is a staunch advocate of Berne's re-parenting process, Dr. Sartin has been extremely successful in implementing change through the use of this technique.

While I prefer a more eclectic approach, my goal and Dr. Sartin's is essentially the same. The object is to change the client's Losing life-script (programming) into a Winner's life-script.

According to Dr. Sartin, the initial process begins with the abandonment of all functional obstacles that obscure the path to winning. One of the primary obstacles is *fear*. Fear is the seed from which all losing is born. From the moment the second person watched the first person die, man was afraid. Even religion's promise of everlasting life has not been enough to appease that fear.

The fact is, all philosophical and scientific theories and advancements since the beginning of time have been created out of the impetus of fear. Fire was discovered to appease man's fear of freezing. Weapons were invented to stave off man's fear of his enemies. Medicine was created as a means of combatting that frightening word—disease. In essence, all fear is based on the ultimate fear—the fear of death. Death represents loss—loss of personal possessions, loss of loved ones, loss of life.

Each day, we are subject to "little deaths." These begin in the form of negative parental injunctions such as "You can't do this," "You can't do that," "You must look for security," "You can't win," "NO!" etc. In the process of being subjected to these little deaths, a little piece of us dies with each injunction. And it gets worse, because we continue to add some of our own personal injunctions—and so, the list continues to grow.

In order to survive, we have learned to adapt to our negative programming. Psychological adaptation was IMPOSED upon us by well-meaning parents, teachers, religious leaders and other adult authority figures. It should be noted that this was *not* done for our personal benefit, but for the benefit of the IMPOSER, even as this person somehow convinced us that what they were doing was "for (our) own good."

Once we have made our psychological adaptation, we tend to live out the life-script of our parents, teachers, religious leaders and other adult authority figures. The adaptation itself can result in a series of unsuccessful life experiences involving personal relationships, health, business, finance, etc.

But that isn't necessarily where it ends. In time, many of us may take on an even more serious form of adaptation—that of the alcoholic, substance abuser, overeater, problem gambler, etc. The foregoing are ALL functions of the same disorder—an unhealthy adaptation of a *losing* life-script.

The primary purpose of this chapter has been to demonstrate how one form of negative adaptation—problem gambling—can be treated and even cured through the concept of Win Therapy, which centers on changing the Losing life-script into a *Winning* life-script. It encompasses a basic truth that can be applied to other areas of life as well—"THE CURE FOR LOSING . . . IS WINNING!"

If you have accepted a Losing life-script, rest assured it can be changed and rewritten from a *Winner's* point of view. How? The answer can be found in Chapter 10—"Creating a Winning Life-Script." In this chapter, a modified model will demonstrate how you can make those all-important changes in your life.

I am happy to say that I have become a Winner at the things I enjoy doing. What about you? Are you ready to create a *Winning* life-script? If so, *just turn to the next page* . . .

CHAPTER 10
Creating A Winning Life-Script

To paraphrase Shakespeare, "Life is but a stage and we are the actors." While Shakespeare, at that time, would not have been familiar with the concept of a life-script, he instinctively knew that we are all actors and actresses in this drama called "Life."

Creating a life-script is our way of "fitting in" or even surviving in this world. But all too often, the role we assume is not of our own making or choosing. The original part was written by our parents and, through the years, is gradually modified or embellished upon by whomever we have come to accept as "authority figures."

What are the roles we act out? Here are a list of some of the more common ones:

Loser	Martyr	People-Pleaser
Helpless One	Prosecutor	Enabler
Perfect One	Rescuer	Rebel
Sufferer	Victim	The Problem

Whatever part we choose, we will continue to act it out until we consciously decide to change it.

At present, your life-script includes all the things your parents ever taught you, and everything else you have ever seen or heard that, in one way or another, helped to create certain perceptions that you now believe to be true.

NOTE: Most of what seems to be happening to you is actually happening *because* of you. You may be sure that the events in your life are presently occurring as a direct result of something you have consciously or unconsciously created, directed or simply allowed to happen. Much of it may well have evolved out of a period in your life when you had little or no voice in the matter.

YOU BELIEVE WHAT YOU HAVE BEEN PROGRAMMED TO BELIEVE

If you have been thinking that your beliefs are genetic, that you were simply born with a predisposition toward a certain kind of thinking, *think again*! The fact is, you believe what you have been programmed to believe. It doesn't matter who did the programming, or whether the messages you received were true or false. It is your *acceptance* of those messages that formulates the basis for your belief system.

The process of rewriting your life-script cannot begin until you are willing to take a closer and more critical look at exactly what it is that you have come to accept. It means rejecting false beliefs in favor of those that are true.

THE POWER OF BELIEFS

In order for us to accept an idea, we need only *believe* that it is true. Beliefs are so powerful that even if they have no basis in reality, our inner *feelings* about them will be enough to motivate us to take a specific course of action.

EXAMPLE: Let us assume that you believe (or feel) that you are inclined to overeat. Perhaps you have been fighting obesity for a number of years and have failed at every diet you have ever tried. Left alone with a box of cookies, do you suppose you will limit yourself to eating only one? Of course not! Your life-script dictates that you must eat the entire box. Why? Because you are an overeater and that is the role that an overeater plays.

Are you beginning to see how powerful your belief system really is? Although you may never have thought it possible, your belief system may presently have you doing all the things you would rather NOT be doing, if you only knew how to stop. Well, now you know how to stop. Just write another script!

Beliefs are nothing more than perspectives from which we view life. In some cases they are true, and in others, they are not. Bear in mind that the subconscious will act on whatever is fed into it. It does NOT examine or critique this information. It simply accepts it AS IS.

INJUNCTIONS AND CONTAMINATED MESSAGES

These are distortions of reality expressed with highly emotional conviction but without any logical basis. Contamination begins from the moment we are born and results from a child's process of adaptation for the purpose of gaining such life-essential needs as parental recognition, love, nurturing and acceptance. The messages themselves often remain long after there is no further need for them.

FORMING A SELF-VIEW

Here we have a viewpoint of ourselves that is born out of the way we think that *others* see us. Based on the feedback we receive, we tend to develop a form of internal dialogue and a perception of reality that is intended to support the feedback we receive. Consider a situation in which a child is repeatedly told that he is stupid or clumsy. Having been programmed in this way, the child will retain these messages and continue to play them out even as an adult.

If your old thought patterns are no longer useful and possibly even self-destructive, why do you suppose that you hold onto them? The answer lies in the basis for *all* our behavior patterns, which, of course, are tied into receiving "strokes" or "rewards." Since early childhood, we have been trained to judge our own self-worth through the degree of acceptance we receive from parental/authority figures.

SORTING OUT THE TRUTH

Since we all act out a life-script which, in time, becomes our individual perception of reality, there is a pressing need to separate the truth from the lies. This can easily enough be accomplished through a five-step process:

1. Take a good hard look at any belief (or mental block) that may be keeping you from doing, being or having whatever it is you desire.

2. Ask yourself WHO has been telling you these so-called "truths" in the first place. Isolate the source!

3. Evaluate this source's *true ability* to make such statements, and to have such a critical influence upon your life. Were the messages themselves coming from factual experience, or were they just the "passing on" of adaptive psychological reasoning? Were the people advising you well-meaning authority figures who were determined to pass on the credo of "right and wrong" that had been passed along to them by previous generations of well-meaning authorities, which didn't have any basis in reality either?

4. Examine what was actually said, and what was truly meant. If you have somehow misinterpreted or misconstrued the message—WHY? Did you hear what was actually said or only what you *wanted* to hear?

5. Ask yourself if your parents' love for you was so limited that you could only retain it by adapting to *their* misconceptions and prejudices.

Bear in mind that hanging on to old beliefs is evidence of an unconscious desire to receive strokes or parental approval.

NOTE: The foregoing questions are designed to help you become more aware of how, why and when you started accepting negative thought patterns that are affecting your present life, and also, your future success.

Freedom can only be realized through a desire to finally "grow up," which means that you are no longer willing to play out the life-script of a child. In actuality, you can only function as an adult when you finally "leave home," or give up the need for parental approval and recognition, as well as the approval and recognition of all *other* authority figures!

REINFORCING THROUGH SELF-DIALOGUE

Throughout our childhoods, the authority figures in our lives programmed us either through contaminated messages or through positive reality-based messages. These came to us in the form of injunctions or commands. In addition, we gradually added our own messages, or internal self-dialogue.

Self-dialogue includes reviewing what has previously happened as well as previewing what we hope or even *fear* might happen. Controlling this inner language is the whole key to changing our life-script. The change itself occurs once we learn to isolate unreality-based negative programming which is then replaced with "turnaround" messages.

EXAMPLE:

PROGRAMMED MESSAGE	TURNAROUND MESSAGE
Today just isn't my day	Today is what I make it
I already know this won't work	This time it WILL work
I never know what to say	I always know what to say
If I only had more time	I can find the time I need
I never win anything	It's my turn to win
The only luck I have is bad luck	I create my own luck
I never get a break	I create my own opportunities
If I only had more education	It's never too late to learn
I don't have the energy I once had	My energy level is increasing daily
If I only had more money	I am rich with money-making ideas
I can't trust anyone	I attract trustworthy people
Nothing seems to go right for me	I am in control of my destiny
I can't seem to get organized	I have incredible organizational ability

If only I could do it over again   I am ready to let go of the
                                      past

As you can see, it is extremely important to analyze negative self-dialogue and to replace it with positive turnaround messages. If you fail to do this, your present life-script will start pulling you off in the wrong direction.

A question you should always ask yourself is: "Although I have been saying this for years, is it really *true*? Is it really true that I _____(you fill in the blank)."

Although you may find it hard to believe, ALL negative statements about yourself are false. You either accepted them as part of your original life-script or have concocted them on your own. In any case, the fact that you have accepted them does NOT make them true!

Remember—whenever you say something negative about yourself, you are creating a negative belief system. Having done this, you will then act out your beliefs as if they were true. And what you hold in your mind is automatically drawn to you, which tends to *reinforce* your negative programming.

SIX NEGATIVE THINKING PATTERNS

ANXIOUS THINKING—Perceiving dangers you feel you won't be able to handle or cope with.

DEPRESSED THINKING—Convincing yourself that you lack the necessary skills to live a happy, well-adjusted life.

OBSESSIVE THINKING—Trapping yourself in a cycle of negative and sometimes illogical reasoning that never seems to resolve itself.

NARCISSISTIC THINKING—An exaggerated self-centeredness or constant preoccupation with yourself.

MASOCHISTIC THINKING—Deriving pleasure from the pain of suffering.

DETACHED THINKING—Suppressing your feelings and believing that "going it alone" is your greatest virtue.

NOTE: Until you clearly identify your negative thinking patterns, you will never be able to change the negative self-dialogue that tends to reinforce them.

FIVE STEPS TO CHANGING NEGATIVE SELF-DIALOGUE

1. LISTEN
Listen attentively to what you are actually saying to yourself.
Do you like what you are hearing? If not, go on to Step 2.
2. LOCATE
Locate the SOURCE of your negative self-dialogue. Where did
it begin? Who told you it was true?
3. STOP
STOP TALKING TO YOURSELF LIKE THAT! When the negative self-messages begin, you have to consciously STOP them.
"If I only had..." "I'll never..." "I can't..." "What if...?" Whenever such ideas begin to form, picture a big red STOP SIGN in
your mind and immediately STOP what you are thinking!
4. REPLACE
Replace the negative thought pattern right then and there. *Now
is the time to correct it!* Don't let it get to the subjective level.
Insist upon thinking for yourself. You are NOT a robot! There is
no reason to blindly accept anything. You always have choices.
Exercise them!
5. REDIRECT
Redirect your turnaround thought toward a positive end result.
Tie it into whatever you are seeking to accomplish. For example:
If it has always been your tendency to say, "I'll never be rich!"
change the message to "I know I can earn enough money doing
(fill in your goal) to meet all my needs."

YOU ARE YOUR FUTURE

If you think that only a psychic can tell you what the future
holds, you are wasting your time and money. You can easily
enough determine your *own* future, just by taking a closer look
at the beliefs you are presently harboring. Whatever they are,
you may be sure they will determine what is going to happen
next.

The human mind is capable of generating images of either

accomplishment or failure. At any given moment, you can hold only one primary belief, one primary feeling and one primary idea. If you seem to be vacillating between two beliefs, feelings or ideas, your subconscious mind will ultimately accept the more dominant one as your reality.

BELIEFS CONTROL FEELINGS AND EMOTIONS

Feelings are what determine motivation. In order to change your behavior, you must first feel motivated to do so. Motivation, in turn, determines actions. What are we actually saying here? Simply this. Feelings not only affect *what* we do but *how* we do it. If our feelings are positive, our actions will be positive as well. But if we are negatively motivated by fear, resentment, anger or frustration, our actions will be negative and self-defeating.

The important thing to remember here is that our feelings are *always* controlled by our beliefs. That being the case, our self-dialogue and self-imagery must be closely monitored at all times in order to insure the most positive outlook on life.

THE END RESULT

The final outcome that results from our thought process is our actual behavior pattern. In other words, the end result is either what we do or *fail* to do. The right series of actions will, of course, produce right results. Conversely, a series of wrong actions can produce only wrong results and overall failure.

Throughout your life, you have undoubtedly asked yourself a number of the following questions: "Why do I do what I do?" "Why don't I do what I should be doing instead of the opposite?" "What makes me act the way I act, behave as I behave?" "Is it that I don't know any better?" "What is wrong with me?" "Why can't I get my act together?"

There is a great amount of truth in the statement *"To know better is not to do better."* The reason it is so difficult for you to make the transition from *knowing* to *doing* is that the life-script you have accepted is now ages old, having been formed by child-hood programming, self-dialogue, beliefs and feelings which, in turn, cause you to act as you do. You cannot do otherwise unless your life-script is changed.

NOTE: How we act not only demonstrates our *view* of life but also our *commitment* to life. Once we understand that our thoughts and actions are irrevocably linked, we are better able to use our minds to accomplish our desires and goals.

RESISTANCE TO CHANGE

Resistance to change is consenting to a fate prescribed by parental/social programming or scripting. Wallowing in negative scripts authored by well-intentioned authority figures provides an excuse for failure and masochistic strokes. Make no mistake about it—your success or failure in life can be directly tied to the life-script you have accepted and are presently acting out.

By saying it is too difficult to change, you are merely erecting a wall of resistance. The reason you do this is that you are reluctant to cut through the old umbilical cord that has always tied you to an adaptive need for parental love, acceptance, recognition and approval.

Now for the good news! The past does not control the future unless you let it. If you want to behave like a seven-year-old child, then that is your choice. No one is *forcing* you to live that way.

Although we are strongly influenced by the experiences in our lives and the things we have been taught, the past only determines our future behavior insofar as we allow it to. Our lives are run by our own design—either consciously or unconsciously.

The choices we make in the present are all that matter. We can either act out the past (play the child) or operate in the present (as an adult). For many of us, it is TIME TO GROW UP!

Realize that your resistance to change is quite normal. Because your subconscious mind is a survival mechanism, it will continue to respond to old programming until a new script has been firmly locked into place.

Realize too that nothing outside of you is responsible for making you what you are. Who you are and what you do is determined by the manner in which you view yourself.

Change becomes easier to accept once you realize that it actually requires more energy to hold on to unworkable, outmoded beliefs than it does to change and to *succeed*!

While change means rejecting the past, it also offers many exciting opportunities for the future. In view of this, I urge you NOT to identify with the kind of self-dialogue that tends to restrict or defeat you.

EXAMPLE: "*I can't help it. That's just the way I AM!*" The truth is, whatever is happening in your life right now is not determined by the way you are, but rather, by the way you have chosen to be.

THE WILL TO CHANGE

Rewriting your life-script begins with the use of the Will. But before one can exercise the power of Will, one must first understand what it is, and how it was meant to be used.

There are many forms of Will. The two we are primarily concerned with here are Good Will and Will Power, since these constitute the most effective tools for change.

Good Will is the power of benevolence. It is our basic acceptance of the fact that we are all truly united on this earth, in the sense that what affects one, affects us all. Hence, the first aspect in recognizing and benefitting from the power of Will is...LOVE.

Love is a powerful universal force that harmonizes, attracts and motivates. Success in life begins with properly loving oneself. It is not until you truly love yourself that you can also love others. Everything you do, every change you initiate will be filtered through the Good Will you feel toward yourself and others. By the same token, it is Good Will that enables you to forgive unconditionally and to excuse the mistakes of the past.

The second use of Will is through Will Power. In essence, Will Power embodies the most vital ingredient of change, which is self-determination. In order to have the Will Power or self-determination to alter your life-script, you must also have the following:

1. A Purpose
2. A Passion
3. A Path

1. YOUR PURPOSE

Your purpose on this earth is your overall reason for being. YOUR LIFE IS AS VALUABLE AS YOU MAKE IT! Life without purpose is fueled by anxiety, frustration and unhappiness. The logical alternative is to create a purpose and lifestyle you truly desire.

In a manner of speaking, your statement of purpose is your general mission in life. It tends to answer the question of "why you are here." It also acts as an overview and guide, moving you past survival needs and restrictive and self-defeating fears. It allows you to have the kind of faith in yourself that is bigger than any obstacle you could possibly encounter.

In determining our purpose for being, we must first determine what it is we truly *love* to do. NOTE: You will not feel a sense of true commitment to anything you do not feel strongly about! The most important aspect of a clearly defined purpose is that it lets us know when we are getting off target. If what you are presently doing is not what you *want* to be doing, then you know it is time for a change.

2. YOUR PASSION

Passion is the way in which we demonstrate our purpose. Passion is expressed through commitment. It is also the path of the heart. Passion is best expressed when we love what we are doing rather than restrict ourselves to what we feel we "should" or "ought" to be doing.

Passion inspires motivation. We will not be commited to change unless we are properly motivated. While there are many forms of motivation, i.e., fear motivation, deficiency motivation and outward motivation, only *inner* motivation will guarantee permanent and lasting success. Why? Because this is motivation from the heart. It is the passion we experience when we become truly excited and enthusiastic about our personal desires and goals.

Finding your true purpose and passion begins with a personal *commitment* to purpose and passion. Take a close look at what motivates you to achieve. Deliberate upon it. Reflect upon it. Keep coming back to that question until you have found a concrete answer. Once you have it, write your answer down as you will need to refer to it later.

3. YOUR PATH

There is a specific path you must take in order to fulfill your purpose. Please understand that a *purpose* and a *goal* are not the same. The major difference between them is that *purpose* is an ongoing event, while *goals* are the steps you take along the way.

The best way to begin is by telling yourself how EASY it is! This thought will quickly become a belief which you will then act upon in order to create the desired end result.

What you will need to get started:

1. A clear VISION of what it is you really want
2. A BELIEF that you can change whatever needs to be changed
3. Practical SKILLS to put that belief into action.

REWRITING YOUR OLD LIFE-SCRIPT

Here is an exercise that will help you to rewrite and redesign your life-script. It will enable you to focus on the things that need to be changed and the best ways in which to change them.

CREATING A WINNING LIFE-SCRIPT

MY OLD SCRIPT:

My PURPOSE was: (Example) To receive love in the form of parental recognition and approval.

My PASSION was: (Example) To be "right" all the time rather than being happy. Being overly compliant to the wishes of others, and rescuing others before taking care of myself.

My PATH was: (Example) Living in the wrong place, working at the wrong job, associating with people who did not add to the quality of my life.

MY NEW SCRIPT:

I, (Your name here) _____, realize that everything I am and everything I do is determined by the programming that I have consciously or unconsciously accepted as my reality. This programming has created my present belief system. Until I change my beliefs, I will continue to act them out in negative and self-defeating ways. I desire to rewrite the life-script that was written for me by others:

My PURPOSE is: (Example) To do what I love and love what I do. To be totally responsible for my own choices, without the need for approval or recognition from others.

My PASSION is: (Example) To involve myself in a professional environment and in personal relationships that make me happy. To achieve excellence in everything I do without the need for perfection.

My PATH is: (Example) To find a new place to live. To change my job and start a new business that is truly aligned with my PURPOSE. To establish healthy relationships with positive people that add to the quality of my life.

MY PLAN OF ACTION IS:

The FIRST thing I am going to do is:

_____

_____

My target date for completion is: _____

The SECOND thing I am going to do is:

_____

_____

My target date for completion is: _____

CONTAMINATED BELIEFS THAT HAVE HELD ME BACK:

_____

_____

_____

MY TURNAROUND THOUGHTS (AFFIRMATIONS) FOR SUCCESS:

_____

_____

_____

I intend to reread my new life-script every morning before I start my day and every evening before I go to sleep so that I can successfully reprogram my subconscious success mechanism. I will do this every day for the next twenty-one days, without skipping a single day!

I am enthusiastic and excited about creating my new life-script since this will enable me to free myself from past nonproductive patterns. I know that this is working for me because I am living proof that my past thoughts and actions have created my present reality. I am willing to do whatever it takes to become the person I want to be and to live the life I want to live. I accept this and expect positive results.

I AM A WINNER!

_____
(Signature)

Dated: _____

CHAPTER 11
Making A Good Luck Wheel Of Fortune To Obtain Your Desires

Many years ago I attended a lecture given by a man known as "Norvell." At that time, he was referred to as the "20th Century Philosopher" and frequently gave lectures to capacity crowds at Carnegie Hall in New York City and at the Wilshire Ebel Theater in Los Angeles.

Norvell was one of the first public speakers to conduct seminars on the subject of creating success through mind power development. He also wrote over twenty-seven books on the subject. His first book, *Meta-Physics—New Dimensions of the Mind*, became a classic best-seller.

I had just finished my Ph.D. work in psychology and was not quite sure which direction I wished to take in the course of pursuing my career. One day I saw an ad in the paper announcing Norvell's seminar, and thinking it might be an interesting experience, I decided to attend.

I remember sitting in the audience, eagerly awaiting this man who was known as the "20th Century Philosopher." When at last he appeared, he was wearing a white suit and began talking to his audience in a voice that was quite deep and theatrical.

I later learned that before becoming a public speaker and involving himself in mind power research, Norvell had been a vaudeville entertainer. Later, he lived in Hollywood, where he became a personal advisor to many Hollywood celebrities, including Howard Hughes. While his theatrical background served him well in captivating an audience, it was also quite apparent that Norvell had thoroughly researched his subject matter.

This was the first time I had ever been exposed to the metaphysical rather than the psychological aspects of the mind. It occurred to me that if these two fascinating fields could somehow be combined, the results would be truly dynamic! With this in mind, I took it upon myself to approach Norvell at the conclusion of his lecture. I asked if I could meet with him that evening, and he immediately agreed, almost as if he already knew what I wished to discuss.

To make a long story short, that was the beginning of my speaking career. I served as Norvell's protégé for a period of three years, during which time I traveled with him and presented my own series of lectures and seminars. Sometimes we worked together. At other times, I worked alone. Norvell not only taught me how to properly "deliver" my message, but also how to utilize what he referred to as "The Good Luck Wheel Of Fortune."

One thing he repeatedly emphasized was the incredible power of mental imagery. After explaining that the mind's creative powers were triggered by images or "mental pictures," he always stressed the importance of properly focusing that power in order to achieve the quickest and most effective results. One of the techniques Norvell regularly employed was The Good Luck Wheel of Fortune.

I soon realized that this was not only a powerful tool, but one that was also a great deal of fun to work with. In actuality, it is a physical picture of a person's desired reality combined with affirmations and a "source" focus. Here is how it looks:

The Good Luck Wheel of Fortune is extremely valuable because it forms a clear, sharp image which can then attract and focus positive energies upon specific desires and goals. In a sense, it is like the blueprint an architect uses in designing a building.

The illustration shown may be copied and adapted to your own use. All you need do is fill it in with appropriate pictures and words cut from various magazines, books, newspapers, drawings, etc. NOTE: It is always best to use colored images since these are

My Good Luck Wheel
of Fortune

Your Name Here

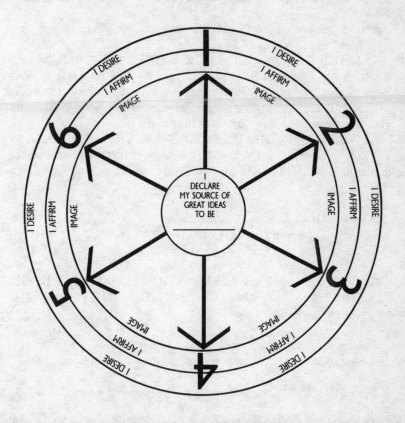

known to have greater power and impact upon your subconscious mind.

I urge you NOT to be fooled by the simplicity of this idea! Although it may seem like a form of child's play, it is actually a powerful magnet that will help you to draw everything good into your life.

While you may be able to create what you want *without* a Wheel of Fortune, using one will cause things to happen that much faster. I know it has worked for me, and I'm sure it will work for you!

Listed below are some helpful suggestions for creating your own Good Luck Wheel of Fortune.

1. MAKE YOUR GOOD LUCK WHEEL OF FORTUNE AS LARGE AS POSSIBLE. It should be at least notebook size. A large poster size is even better, particularly if you have the room to mount it on a wall. The larger the size of the wheel, the more you will tend to focus your attention upon it.

2. WRITE YOUR DESIRES (GOALS) IN THE SPACES NEXT TO THE NUMBERS. Example: In the space next to No. 1, where it reads, "I DESIRE," you may wish to write in one of the following:

A new or used (name of automobile)
To earn $1,000 in the next 60 days
To meet someone who can assist me with...

3. WRITE DOWN AN AFFIRMATION FOR YOUR DESIRE. Example: In the space where it reads, "I AFFIRM," you may wish to write in one of the following:

I attract the right automobile at the right price
A new money-making opportunity to earn $1,000 is available
   to me
I am attracted to someone who will assist me with...

As you will see, affirmations, when properly used, are powerful tools for manifesting your desires. The word affirmation means to "firm up." By using positive statements, you are "firming up" your expectancy of desired end results.

You will notice that affirmations are always phrased in a positive way. It is important to affirm what you DO want, not what you DON'T want. It is not very inspiring to voice the affirmation

"I don't want to be broke." Instead, you should affirm that you will create a money-making opportunity that brings you all the money you need.

When properly phrased, your affirmations will motivate you to take ACTION! This means you are no longer willing to wait for something to happen, you are ready to MAKE things happen!

The affirmations listed above strongly imply that you will attract your desires, which simply means that you will take positive steps to find what you are looking for. Affirming that a money-making opportunity is open to you implies that you are not expecting to win a lottery, but that you are open to any opportunity that will enable you to earn the money you desire.

Look at your Good Luck Wheel of Fortune and repeat your affirmations at least twice daily—once in the morning, and once at night.

4. PLACE IMAGES OF YOUR DESIRES OR GOALS ON YOUR GOOD LUCK WHEEL OF FORTUNE. Place illustrations of some sort—a photo, or possibly a picture out of a magazine, in the spaces provided. If your desire is somewhat abstract, select an image that tends to *suggest* the desired end result—anything that will help you to make the connection in your mind.

Examples:

A color photo of the automobile you desire
A picture of a $1,000 bill or ten $100 bills
A picture or drawing of someone doing what you want this person to assist you with

The significant thing here is to show your desire in a completed form. Do not use images of *how* you are going to accomplish the end result, since if you do, you will limit yourself. Leave it up to the subconscious mind to figure out How.

5. WRITE A DEFINITION OF YOUR CREATIVE SOURCE. Write down the name or definition of the "source" of your creative ideas. It could be a religious name, or possibly just the words "Infinite Source." Whatever it is, this is the source from which everything is formed. It is extremely important to acknowledge and remind yourself that all good luck comes from an Infinite Source that works through your mind.

6. WRITE DOWN A COMPLETION DATE. Write down a specific date on which you expect to complete a project, fulfill a desire

or reach a goal. Until your subconscious has been trained to respond to this process, it may take a little longer than expected. In any case, allow *at least* twenty-one days to complete whatever it is you intend to do.

7. LOOK AT YOUR GOOD LUCK WHEEL OF FORTUNE AS OFTEN AS POSSIBLE. Mount your Good Luck Wheel of Fortune in a conspicuous place where you are sure to see it many times each day. Each time you look at it, you will be programming your subconscious with strong visual images which will quickly go to work for you.

8. INCREASE RESULTS WITH MENTAL IMAGERY. Use Mental Imagery to speed up the manifestation of your desires. We think and create through mental images, so, in addition to reviewing the information on your Good Luck Wheel of Fortune, take a few moments and close your eyes. Start with Desire No. 1 and just "see" yourself experiencing the desired end result.

Make sure that YOU are in the picture. Again, you should attempt to observe the scene in completed form. Since we all tend to think in images, and since our minds are teleological, they will begin to draw us toward whatever we picture with ever-increasing intensity.

There is nothing magical about the Good Luck Wheel of Fortune, nor can it be classified as a form of superstition or wishful thinking. Rather, it is based on a scientifically sound principle which assures us that the mind *will* respond and cause us to move toward and ultimately create any image we focus upon. The Good Luck Wheel of Fortune can greatly assist you here, since it enables you to clarify the desired end result so that your mind has a crystal-clear picture of your intention.

STIMULATING YOUR C.M.I.

In case you haven't figured it out by now, the primary purpose of the Good Luck Wheel of Fortune is to stimulate your C.M.I. (Creative Mental Imagery).

Every creation begins with an idea—an image. The subconscious mind is stimulated to *action* or *completion* through images. In Gestalt psychology there is a concept known as "closure." In regard to imaging, it works like this:

The subconscious mind goes into a state of anxiety if there is a conflict between what we *have* and what we *want*. It is always in the process of trying to resolve the conflict between our thoughts and images with what we actually have in our physical reality. It works around the clock, even when we are sleeping, to *close the gap* or *resolve the conflict*.

The reason C.M.I. and the Good Luck Wheel of Fortune work is that they increase our anxiety in a *positive manner* by creating discontent within the subconscious, which stimulates your subconscious to create whatever you focus your attention on.

As you look at the images and repeat the affirmations on your Good Luck Wheel of Fortune, you immediately set up a conflict in your mind. For example, if you are focusing on a certain amount of money while you are broke, the subconscious must go to work to resolve the conflict in your mind.

Since the subconscious mind can't tell the difference between a real or an imagined experience, it thinks that you are rich because you are constantly programming it with thoughts and images of riches. As you keep reinforcing the image of riches, the conflict or anxiety builds until your subconscious finds a way to resolve it. You will then be led to ways in which you can manifest the riches you have been focusing on and imaging through the use of the Good Luck Wheel of Fortune.

All of this happens *without any effort on your part*. Your success depends upon your willingness to hold onto the thoughts and images that support your final goal. Your marvelous subconscious success-producing mechanism has no choice but to lead you to the people, circumstances and conditions to complete the closure between what you have and what you want. So, I urge you not to underestimate the Good Luck Wheel of Fortune. Let it work *for* you!

INTENTION—THE POWER BEHIND YOUR GOOD LUCK WHEEL OF FORTUNE

Quite simply, the Good Luck Wheel of Fortune encompasses three vital elements of the creative process: DESIRE, BELIEF and EXPECTANCY Actually, you could sum up these three words in a *single* word: INTENTION. Intention is your desired end result. The clearer you are on your intention, the faster you will be able to achieve your end result.

Intention sets the laws of mind (the operation of the conscious, subconscious and superconscious) into motion. Your intention is what positions the Good Luck Wheel of Fortune so that chance opportunities are presented to you to complete your desired end result.

"THIS OR SOMETHING BETTER"

We sometimes desire things that are not in our best interests. In many cases, there is something *better* available to us, which we may not be aware of.

With this in mind, it is best to complete your mental imagery exercise (Step No. 5) with the following statement: "*I accept this or something better!*"

In every instance, it is wise to hold onto your goals lightly, even if you think they are the only ones that are ideally suited to you. When you have a heavy emotional investment riding on a specific outcome, you often *force* things to happen. Then too, you will be extremely upset if things do not turn out exactly as planned.

Meanwhile, your subconscious may be trying to alert you to an outcome with far greater potential which you will fail to see once you become too focused on a specific end result.

It is important to be mentally flexible and to make the necessary changes to bring about the perfect end result. Should you get the nagging (intuitive) feeling that some changes are in order, all that is necessary is to change your mental images and your Good Luck Wheel of Fortune accordingly.

DISCOVERING WHAT YOU WANT

The Good Luck Wheel of Fortune can also be useful in helping you to discover what you want. Quite often people are not sure what they want but would know it if they saw it or were exposed to it.

A few years ago I met a man in a Las Vegas casino. His name

was John. John made his living as an electronics repairman. His hobby was traveling to Las Vegas to enter the slot machine tournaments. He told me that he would compete against other players who all started with the same bankroll. The person who had the most money after a specific period of time and play was officially declared the winner. Personally, I think slot machines are a fast way to part with your money, but John actually made a profit on the tournaments.

As he and I continued to talk, I glanced toward a nearby roulette wheel and casually mentioned that it reminded me of something I had devised called the Good Luck Wheel of Fortune. When John asked me to explain what it was, I told him it was a mental and visual process for focusing the subconscious on producing a desired end result. "Of course," I said, "it *helps* to know what you want."

"Unfortunately," John responded, "that rules me out. I've never been the type to know what I want. I enjoy what I do for a living, but I think there must be something more interesting to do. I've always envied people who seemed to have their sights set since the age of nine or ten. It must be wonderful to be that focused and that certain about things. As for me, well, I have some vague ideas, but nothing I'm really zeroed in on. Your Good Luck Wheel of Fortune really intrigues me, although I don't know how I would ever use it. Oh well, I suppose it can't work for everybody. I only wish it could. It sounds like a lot of fun."

"I think the Good Luck Wheel of Fortune could work for you," I insisted, "just in a different way. If you are open to suggestion, John, there is something I would like you to do."

Noticing the receptivity in his eyes, I went ahead and outlined my plan.

"For the next twenty-one days, I would like you to clip out items or pictures from various newspapers and magazines that hold some special significance for you, capturing both your eye and your mind. Take a few moments to examine and think about every item you clip out. At first you will have a random collection of things, but as time goes on, a pattern should gradually emerge. I believe this technique will demonstrate where your greatest powers and interests lie. Eventually, you will know what you want and will be able to use the Good Luck Wheel of Fortune to help you acquire it in the shortest possible time."

The next time I talked to John, which was about six months later, he was extremely excited. I knew, even before he told me, that some major changes had occurred in his life.

"You were right, Dr. Anthony," he said, with great enthusiasm. "I've been clipping out items, just as you asked me to do, and one day I realized that most of them had to do with either electronics or playing the slot machines. It got me to wondering if there was any possible way of combining the two. With some further research, I found several companies in Nevada that sold used slot machines. Where I come from, slot machines are illegal for gambling purposes. However, they are legal for home or private use. To make a long story short, I opened a store that sells antique and modern restored slot machines. Since I have an electronics background, it wasn't hard for me to learn how to repair them. Business is fantastic, and I'm doing something I really enjoy! In addition, I've put together several 'junkets' and taken people from where I live over to Las Vegas to the slot machine tournaments. I can even write off the expenses on my business. I owe it all to you because your Good Luck Wheel of Fortune helped me to focus on what I wanted to do and gave me the inspiration to search out the connections to make it all possible."

THE MORE YOU USE IT, THE MORE YOU WILL WANT TO USE IT

As you can see, anything is possible if you have the means, the knowledge and commitment. The Good Luck Wheel of Fortune is designed to accelerate the manifestation of your desires. Give it a chance and I can guarantee you that *the more you use it, the more you will WANT to use it*!

CHAPTER 12
What To Do When Your Ship Comes In

If you have successfully applied all the winning techniques in this book, if you have worked hard, with an unshakable sense of dedication and resolve, you are certainly entitled to your reward. The question is, are you also prepared?

For as long as the realization of one's dream remains a long-range goal, it is an easy thing to live with. Life goes along in a familiar and ordinary way. There are no major adjustments to be made. It is simply a matter of getting up each day and working toward a clearly defined objective.

Most people give little or any thought to success until it finally happens. On a grand scale, it can be a truly earth-shaking experience, but only if you haven't properly prepared yourself for it.

Let's consider a few of the things that generally occur when a person's ship finally comes in.

The first reaction is usually "I can't believe this is true!" In situations where a person's success is brought about by his own diligent efforts, it is hardly a logical statement. If you have worked hard, have done everything necessary to achieve your goals, is there really any reason why you shouldn't be successful? Of course not! But there is still an aura of unreality connected with any huge success, perhaps because people inherently expect so little from life.

The next most typical reaction might be even more difficult to understand. In many cases, people are inclined to feel "I don't deserve it." What I have always found intriguing about this is that people rarely adopt such an attitude when something *bad* happens. They seem inclined to accept adversity as their due, but something *really good* is often hard to handle. While people with a high sense of self-esteem may have less trouble accepting the good things that come their way, even they have been known to experience some twinges of doubt.

At this point, superstitious feelings often enter the picture, causing a person to feel that "this can't possibly last!" Believing that something or someone is going to come along and "snatch it all away" is only another way of saying, "I don't deserve it." Although this belief has no actual basis in fact, it is yet another of the more common reactions to success.

What happens after that? Well, that really depends upon you. Let's review a number of the things that CAN happen, both good and bad, and the best ways in which to cope with them.

TRYING TO BE
WHO YOU'VE ALWAYS BEEN

Do you like yourself as a person? Are you comfortable with who you are, content with the way you think and conduct yourself? Then, why change?

Extremely successful people often feel they have a role to play. Society assumes that they will now live in a certain way, drive certain cars, wear certain clothes, belong to private clubs and associate with those whose income bracket is similar to their own. The faulty premise in this line of thinking is that all of us want the same things in life.

How would you like to own a 325-foot yacht, with a mosaic swimming pool, an office, huge master bedroom, semicircular bath and nine guest cabins? Aristotle Onassis owned such a yacht, the largest in all the world. It required a staff of sixty people to keep it properly maintained.

Not surprisingly, most people would love to vacation on such a yacht, but few would have any real interest in assuming the responsibilities of ownership.

If you are a person who has always enjoyed a simple, uncomplicated life, there is no reason why personal success should force you to give that up. But don't be surprised if others *expect* you to give it up, and even belittle your efforts to keep things on an even keel.

One woman I interviewed admitted that she had enjoyed astounding success in the field of commercial real estate. Once she had enough money to retire, she decided instead to open a little antiques shop which she operates with the help of only one part-time employee.

"No one could understand why I would want to spend long hours in this quaint little shop when I could be lying around on a beach in the Bahamas," she said. "The thing is, I truly *love* antiques! The historical significance of each piece is something I enjoy sharing with my clientele. Since the part-time employee I've hired is less knowledgeable on the subject, I feel I need to be in the store as much of the time as possible in order to answer questions and to provide all necessary information. I don't really think of it as a job. Since antiques have always been a hobby of mine, it is more like *playing* at something I've always wanted to do."

I could certainly identify with much of what this woman was saying since I had gone through many similar experiences of my own. In a previous book, *Doing What You Love and Loving What You Do*, I described a period when it became necessary to simplify my lifestyle, to adopt a way of living and being that was more in keeping with the person I actually was. At the time, I remember that some of the changes caused friends and family to feel uneasy and anxious, but this did not deter me from doing what I believed was necessary to live as happily and as honestly as I could.

HOW TO AVOID THE GUILT TRIP

Once you become truly successful, there will be others who envy you. Envy is not a feeling that anyone enjoys experiencing since it is always tied into the nagging reminder that someone else is doing *better*. Envy will often cause people to make you feel guilty about what you have. Suddenly, you will find yourself inundated with the latest statistics on those who are destitute and living in the streets. Notwithstanding your own desire to help such people, which you can certainly do through any number of charitable endeavors, there is no reason to feel guilty about having something that others do not. You *earned* what you have, and that gives you the right to have it. By the same token, you are in a far better position to help others less fortunate if you, yourself, are successful.

Moral of the Story: You should always be proud of your achievements, not ashamed! And never allow yourself to be affected by the envy or jealousy of others. They are free to enjoy many accomplishments and successes of their own, once they make up their minds to it!

THE MONEY TRAP

It is indeed unfortunate that so many people see money as a "trap," as something that is destined to affect their lives in some undesirable way. The way to avoid any possibility of this is to decide at the outset that you are going to control your money, your money is not going to control you.

If money is allowed to become your master, it will soon have you doing some "wild and crazy" things. Although it is easy to get carried away with the exhilarating feeling that comes with greater financial strength, there is no reason to allow this feeling to get out of control. A part of what you earn should always be allocated to sound investments, which means that you MUST adhere to a "hands off" policy toward that portion of your income. As long as you are looking toward the future in a practical and realistic way, you will never be hurt by a few extravagances in the present. The answer lies in maintaining a good balance between spending and saving.

NEITHER A GEYSER
NOR A MISER BE

A geyser, as we all know, is a natural gusher that periodically spews forth boiling hot water or steam. As your fortunes continue to increase, it would be best not to think of yourself as a *financial geyser*, a source of endless monetary wealth, since your fortunes can always reverse themselves. By the same token, there is absolutely no reason to live like a miser, someone who is inclined or even determined to live *beneath* his means.

Those afflicted with a chronic case of poverty-thinking find it impossible to increase their spending habits once good fortune comes their way. They continue to pinch pennies, to save for a rainy day, to wait for some catastrophic event to occur. The memory of earlier, more difficult times continues to haunt them. What happened before could happen again. Perhaps it is even inevitable!

Even if you are *not* plagued with such thoughts, you may still be a victim of poverty consciousness since it is known to manifest itself in many ways.

Do you hate to spend money on yourself? If you find it easier to spend money on others, you may be afflicted with yet another form of poverty consciousness.

Other signs often include a tendency to put off making purchases, and an inability to decide what you really want.

Respect yourself enough to know that you deserve what you want! If at first you find this difficult to do, imagine the universe as a constant source of plenty. The fact is, you are surrounded by more money-making opportunities, more sources of endless supply than you could ever avail yourself of! What you choose *not* to recognize nonetheless exists!

How many people have you known who have made, lost and *remade* a fortune in the space of a single lifetime? I have personally known people who have gone through two or three bankruptcies and then made a million dollars again! Do you think such a thing would be possible if the universal source of unlimited supply were actually *limited*? Or if it was selective in who it chose to shine down upon? Or if it allocated only one fortune to each individual on earth? Fortunately, we have as many opportunities as we care to avail ourselves of.

NOTE: A very vital part of winning is knowing how to lose. Notice that I did not say "fail" since you have not failed if something you attempt goes wrong. You only fail when you never attempt to do anything at all. Losing is an entirely different matter. Losing simply means that you will not always win, although the possibility of winning continues to exist.

SUFFERING FROM THE "SUCCESS SYNDROME"

If you were to talk to any professional psychiatrist, you would soon learn that the Success Syndrome is so common that it is frequently the reason people end up lying on a couch when they would rather be lying on a beach.

Many of the problems associated with success have already been discussed in the foregoing pages, but there is another that frequently afflicts those who have finally "made it big." Inside themselves, successful people often feel they are *frauds*. If you were to ask them why, they would say, "Because I know any number of people who could have done this better. Given the same opportunities, the same breaks—why, they could easily have shown me up with achievements far greater than my own."

For purposes of simplification, let us suppose that you have written a book. It is a book on a subject that you know extremely well. Let us assume it is a How-To book—how to do something or other. Because you are so well-versed on this particular subject, the book itself took you less than six months to complete. It is published by a major house and because of an aggressive advertising campaign and international distribution rights, it quickly becomes a best-seller.

At the time this happens, there is someone living next-door to you who has been working on the Great All-American Novel for a period of seven years. The author has done a monumental amount of research and has submitted several sample chapter packages to various publishers, who have rejected all of his early versions. The book itself has been revised a total of five times. Your next-door neighbor is obviously a hard-working and dedicated individual. From all indications, he deserves to succeed. To make it even worse, he seems delighted with your success as a published author, although you find it difficult to seriously accept yourself in this light. In your own mind, you feel that you only had this one book in you, and that your neighbor has countless volumes.

Is life being fair? Yes, in all probability, it is. To begin with, it is impossible to compare the two books since that would be like comparing apples and oranges. One is an instructional text, and the other, a complex fictional saga covering three generations. As far as research is concerned, it may seem to you that your neighbor has been burdened with the greater portion, but let's take a second look!

The book that you have written has to do with a business in which you have been engaged for a period of twenty-five years. You know this business like the back of your hand. You have seen it through all of its ups and downs, through periods of dramatic change and advancement, and through it all, you have managed to compete successfully in the market. That is the research that YOU have done! It has taken a major portion of your life. For that matter, it has taken much *more* than that. There have been times when it required some daring and risk, when long hours of overtime took you away from your wife and children. Even so, you persevered—and won. That is what YOUR book is about. It also tells your reader how he can avoid many of the pitfalls that you were forced to contend with. The information and helpful advice contained in this volume could save your reader countless hours of time and a great deal of money. Because this message has obviously gotten across, the book has become extremely popular in a relatively short period of time, and *deserves* to be!

The next time you give a helpful bit of advice to someone, stop and think how long it took you to learn the information you have just passed on. Yes, it has value. It has worth.

Just as you have!

ACHIEVING "INNER SUCCESS"

Successes in life can be many and varied. There are both outer and inner successes. Outwardly, it is possible to do great things and to be richly rewarded—both monetarily and through public adulation. Inwardly, success is an altogether different kind of thing. And so are the rewards.

As you continue to work toward your goals, it is necessary to keep *working on yourself*. This means rejecting ideas that are uesless and uninspiring in favor of those that can help you to become a better YOU.

In time, you will come to see the difference between excitement that is aroused by external events and the unique kind of elation that comes from seeking and finding the Truth.

Truth, like Realism, is what it IS. It cannot be affected by anything you think, or say, or do. It will not bend to your will, nor will it become what you would *like* it to be. Truth is Truth.

A comical little filler piece I once read in a magazine made the following observation: *What men usually ask of God when they pray is that two and two NOT make four.*

There is a great deal of *truth* in this, although we might prefer to believe that we do not really think in ways that are illogical, or possibly even *irrational*. Unfortunately, we do! At such times, we frequently find ourselves praying (or wishing) that a problem could simply be *eradicated* from our lives. Or else, that we could be transported ahead to some future time when everything would be "magically resolved."

What do such thoughts have to do with being logical or reasonable? Whatever the problem, you may be sure it came about through a certain combination of circumstances and events, and that it can only be removed by *altering* those circumstances and events in a logical and systematic way.

To become more "inwardly successful" means, among other things, that you will no longer depend upon a "stroke of luck" or any form of "magical intervention" to rescue you from the situation at hand. By the same token, you will no longer be a slave to exterior events. What happens or *doesn't* happen will not make or break you.

NOTE: It is success in the *inner* world that will enable you to place the outer world under your command.

HOW TO ESTABLISH AN ONGOING SUCCESS PROGRAM

You would like success to be ongoing, wouldn't you? In that case, you will have no time to "rest on your laurels" although you might occasionally feel entitled to do so.

This is not the time to "ride the tide" of past achievements. This is the time to think ahead, both in terms of inner and outer success.

What IS success really? Why, success is *enjoying life*! There can be no truer definition. Imagine going to work each day and earning an exorbitant salary for doing something you hate to do. Many people are presently engaged in such occupations. Perhaps you have even known a few. Have you noticed how their inner dissatisfaction has begun to spill over into their personal lives? How it is affecting their loved ones? Obviously, success is not money. Not in itself!

Success has a lot to do with career choices and long-range goals that complement your personal interests and talents. While many people have no trouble deciding what they should do when the question is presented to them in such terms, others remain indecisive.

Perhaps you have heard people say, "When it comes to success, I don't really know what I want. One minute it's one thing, the next minute it's something else."

Success, among other things, is a matter of establishing priorities, of putting *first things first*. As you may already have guessed, the "first things" have more to do with your inner life than your outer life. Why? Because it is impossible to enjoy any of your possessions until you have learned how to thoroughly enjoy yourself! Makes sense, doesn't it?

While there is nothing wrong with having lots of money, it is more important to have an inner peace and serenity with which to greet each day. And while you may have been thinking of totally redesigning your home, it would be far better to work at redesigning the way you think. Yes, there is always some room for improvement there!

An Ongoing Success Program—both inner and outer. It is a vital component of your Winning Life-Script and should never be neglected or ignored. In order to keep going, it is necessary to keep growing!

BECOMING A MAGNET FOR GOOD

While you were busily climbing the ladder of success, you undoubtedly gave considerable thought to acquiring the "good things" in life. Have you ever stopped to think of *yourself* as one of those "good things"?

Do you feel that the world is a better place because you are here? Because of the contributions you have made? Because of the example you have set for others?

Life is a mirror. You get out of it what you put into it. Do you feel that the image you presently reflect could be improved upon, either in your own eyes, or in the eyes of others?

Remember always that your thoughts and words *create*. Whatever you say, or think about, or do, is bound to have some long-range effect, in much the same way that pebbles dropped into a stream create ever-widening rings on the surface of the water.

It is important that we constantly guard our thoughts and words, constantly affirm love, truth and the highest good within ourselves.

What have you been thinking and talking about today? Have you been conveying positive or negative messages? In either case, you can be sure that someone was listening, and reacting to them.

When you were a child, your parents undoubtedly impressed upon you how important it was to live up to Your Word. In affect, your word was a *verbal contract*. Whatever you promised to do might as well have been written in stone since you were always expected to honor your word, live up to it, make good on it. This, of course, is not an easy thing to do if you are constantly saying things that are in contradiction with something you said earlier. Or if you are expressing other people's opinions rather than your own. Or if you are saying things "off the top of your head" that you really have no intention of following through on. If you really *listen* to what you are saying, you may realize that it is time to do some "mental housecleaning."

I once knew an elderly lady who had adopted a somewhat innovative approach to her annual spring cleaning. She would go through her closets and drawers and carefully examine everything that was there. Anything she found that hadn't been used in a year was immediately discarded. This kept her from accumulating needless items that would never be of any use to her. Since she was an elderly woman, I was quite impressed with her unique approach to housecleaning since most of the elderly people I knew were more inclined to *collect* things than to dispose of them.

It occurred to me that a "mental housecleaning" could be accomplished in much the same way, although it would be necessary to do it much more frequently than once a year.

Depending upon what they are, your words are constantly attracting or repelling. They are constantly helping to defeat or inspire others. They are constantly creating positive or negative images that others will tend to judge you by. Your words, of course, are a product of your thoughts, and that is why it is so important to engage in regular "mental housecleaning."

If you wish to draw good into your life, you must first exude it to others. Whatever is truly *good* is beneficial not only to you, but to everyone around you. It is what makes each day a happy, loving and life-enriching experience.

That is success of the Highest Order. Enjoy it! And remember to pass it on!

CHAPTER 13
Ten Attributes All Winners Have In Common

We have discussed the three personality types—Winners, Losers and Non-Winners—quite extensively throughout this book. Once again, let's clarify our definitions:

Winners are individuals who take responsibility for their actions, and who are accustomed to achieving what they want.

Losers are individuals who do not have what they want but have good reasons or excuses for their lack of success or "bad luck".

Non-Winners, for whom this book was written, are individuals who want to be Winners but who lack the necessary knowledge and skills to make the transition.

At this juncture, I think you will agree that you have been exposed to many new ideas and methods that will enable you to make the transition from Non-Winner to Winner. For purposes of review and clarification, I would like to point out some significant attributes that ALL Winners have in common. The list could be much longer, but the ten attributes listed here are the most common, and also, the most essential.

If you are a Non-Winner, you may recognize some of these attributes in yourself. If so—good! If not, you can begin developing them now that you know what they are. As always, winning starts with beginning!

1. A WINNER makes commitments.
   A LOSER makes promises.
If you do not yet have what you want in life, it simply means

that you are not committed to it 100 percent. At some point, you must make a firm commitment, if only to yourself. The difference between a promise and a commitment is that a promise does not generate *action*. It is also something that can easily be broken. We have all heard of broken promises. Commitment, on the other hand, is a guarantee by the person committing to take action and to follow through.

One of the most effective methods of commitment involves making a declaration of your commitment to someone else. This will give you the feeling of being accountable to someone other than yourself. Afterward, even if you are inclined to let yourself "off the hook," others will tend to hold you to your word, or at the very least, continue to remind you of whatever it is you committed yourself to.

The surest path to losing is lack of commitment. As a Winner, you must cease making empty promises that can be broken, and start making commitments that you will hold yourself accountable for.

2. A WINNER says: "Let's find out."
   A LOSER says: "Nobody knows."

The first day I walked into the public library, it suddenly occurred to me that knowledge was at my disposal. I was totally awed by the prospect of visiting the many worlds contained in the books that were there. How comforting it was to know that this reliable source of information actually existed, and that it was all FREE!

In addition to knowledge that comes to us through libraries, there is also an unlimited source of knowledge available through teachers, mentors and specialty information services. In view of this, there is absolutely no reason why we cannot obtain the knowledge we need to succeed.

A Winner continues to strive for excellence in his chosen field, and is always searching for additional information that will enhance his chances of success. Winners have an instinct for surrounding themselves with other knowledgeable people, realizing that in order to succeed it is not necessary, or even possible, to know everything there is to know in their chosen field of endeavor.

Winners search out role models and mentors and avail themselves of their knowledge and experience. If you desire to be a Winner, you MUST learn how to do this! Whatever you need to know or learn, there is somebody, somewhere who has the knowledge, information and experience you are looking for.

Don't accept the Loser's view that "Nobody knows." *Somebody* knows. Find them! Hire them, if you can. At the very least, get into the habit of associating with such people.

Remember the words of the Great Teacher—"Ask, and it shall be given you; seek, and ye shall find; knock, and it shall be opened unto you." I believe that says it all!

3. A WINNER sees an answer in every problem.
   A LOSER sees a problem in every answer.

Winners look for answers. They realize that life is full of problems and that they will either be part of the problem or part of the answer.

If you understand what a problem is, you will understand its true purpose in your life. A problem is simply an obstacle between where you are and where you want to be. When you *master* a problem, you have reached the next rung up the ladder of enlightenment. Each step takes you a little closer to the top, and along the way, you are learning how to transform obstacles into opportunities.

Think back to the last time you were forced to face a truly difficult problem. Before it occurred, you undoubtedly had no idea what you would do if such a thing happened to you. But after it did, you learned something about yourself—and not only about *yourself*, but about the problem as well.

If you were to ask people what they fear most, some typical answers might include "bankruptcy," "illness" or "loss of a loved one." You have probably known people who have survived such experiences, and perhaps you have been through them yourself. If so, then you know that a problem can either be viewed as an obstacle that will immobilize you, or as an opportunity that will enable you to become more self-sufficient and self-confident. Depending upon which end you are approaching it from, it is either the worst possible thing that could happen, or it was a learning experience that taught you some new survival skills that you now consider invaluable.

That's the way it is with problems. You will always have them, but each one has its own solution built into it. If you look closely enough, you will find the answer . . . and a great deal more. Each problem you solve increases your potential for winning.

4. A WINNER says, "I will!" and succeeds.

A LOSER says, "I'll try" and fails.

At the outset, it is important to understand that you will **never** fail because you cannot *do* something. You can only fail if you "try" to do it.

The concept of "trying" has a built-in failure mechanism. To better understand this, I would like you to look around you and find a small object. Now, "try" to pick it up! Did you pick it up? If so, you did not "try." You *actually picked it up*! The bottom line is you either DO something or you DON'T do it. *There is nothing in between.* "Trying" is DECIDING to do something. It is *not* the same as DOING it. What most people call "trying" is actually *not doing* something.

Trying is man's invention. Actually, no such action exists. If trying worked, everyone would be successful because almost everyone will tell you that they're "trying their best." What they don't realize is that as long as they "try," they will continue to fail. The reason for this is simple. Trying violates the basic principle of creation, which is that *we must accept something in mind before we can create it.* When you are "trying," you have not *accepted* that what you want to do, or have, *is already yours*. Therefore, your subconscious mind cannot *act* on it because it has not been programmed into your mental computer. Remember, everything that is created or accomplished was an *accepted idea* in someone's mind first.

Trying also provides an excuse for not getting what you want. It's a "weasel" word with a built-in escape mechanism to excuse failure. Since it's impossible to "try," I would strongly suggest that you remove the word from your vocabulary. Whenever you find yourself saying "I'll try," *stop right there* and substitute "I will!" Remember, you either WILL or you WON'T. You either DO or you DON'T. Just keep in mind: "Tryin' is lyin'."

5. A WINNER is not afraid to be "wrong."

A LOSER has a compulsive need to be "right."

The need to be "right," and the fear of being "wrong," can be traced to 99 percent of all failures in life. The pathology behind this is that when I am right I am "okay." When I am wrong I am "not okay."

We have been taught to look at our mistakes and that that determines what kind of people we are. If we make a lot of mistakes, we are either "stupid" or "bad." On the other hand, if we make few mistakes, we will be viewed as smart, competent and "good."

In an effort to be okay, we tend to reject any action that will make us appear "wrong" and take on any action or activity that makes us appear to be "right." The real problem here is that most people would rather be "right" than happy. In other words, we would rather have the "right" reasons why we can't be a Winner, than take some "wrong" actions that may show that we are actually not a Winner.

Freedom lies in our ability to make it okay to make mistakes. However, we cannot be free to make mistakes if we continue to identify with our actions. We have to learn that we are *not* what we *have* and we are *not* what we *do*. Our actions are the *result* of our thinking, but they are *not who we are*. If we change our thought patterns, we will automatically change our actions. So, we must learn to separate the doer from the deed. As long as we identify with our actions, we will continue to try to be "right."

By now, you have undoubtedly made a few mistakes in your life. You may not remember them all, but you probably remember those that really taught you something. What did you learn? Do you think it was *worth* learning? Of course it was! The purpose of mistakes is to learn what NOT to do. Sometimes this is the only way we can learn WHAT to do.

Learning of any kind is accomplished through trial and error. For the most part, life requires that we operate spontaneously, on the basis of immediate circumstances. Rarely, is there time to advance-test a particular approach to a problem, and of course, we have no guarantees. So, we do the best we can based on our present level of awareness. Sometimes we are right and sometimes we are wrong. *Either way, it's okay!*

I have known a number of individuals who have been so mentally traumatized by an event (mistake) in their life, such as a divorce or bankruptcy, that they would never again trust their own judgment on anything! Such people have not yet learned how to profit from their mistakes. Instead, they tend to retreat into their shell, and therefore, as Thoreau once said, live lives of "quiet desperation."

Their path to freedom, to becoming a Winner, lies in their ability to realize that YOU CAN'T FAIL AS A PERSON. Your business may fail, your relationships may fail, your finances may fail, but there is no way that YOU can fail as a person. All that needs to be done to go from Loser to Winner is to separate the doer from the deed, the actor from the play, and to realize that it is okay to make mistakes and to be "wrong." Rather than blame yourself, correct the thought that produced the mistake and you will never make it again.

6. A WINNER believes that we make our own "luck," either through what we do or what we *fail* to do.
A LOSER believes in "bad luck."

We have learned that "Good Luck," the so-called symbol of winning, achieving and prospering, is actually the result of *right thinking* and *right action*. What is commonly called "bad luck" is nothing more than a misunderstanding and misuse of the powers of the mind.

Our life is a walking, living example of our beliefs. The lucky person is one who thinks and acts like a lucky person. Winners are lucky because they understand how to create good luck and good fortune. They are not surprised when they are lucky, they just accept it as a normal result of their Winner life-script.

The truth is that anyone can be lucky. Our luck is determined by what we do or fail to do. Most importantly, it requires that we have faith and belief in our ability to succeed.

People in the entertainment field have been known to say, "After twenty-five years of hard work, I was suddenly an overnight success." While this is obviously a facetious remark, it is amazing how few adoring fans even realize it. All too often, the attainment of superstardom is thought to eradicate all those early years of struggle. In this, we have the basis for so many unrealistic views of "luck" and "success."

We prefer to believe that what comes hard to us, other people simply "fall into." These "lucky others" always seem to be in the right place at the right time. They appear to have been born with a privileged advantage. In fact, some believe that they were born under a "lucky star," astrologically speaking. Well, if you really believe this, you'll believe anything!

If you want to be a "lucky person," you must understand that everything that happens to you *begins* with you and *ends* with you. There is nothing haphazard, coincidental or circumstantial on the path to winning. The magnificent stream of Universal Consciousness is forever flowing, always attracting like to like.

You are responsible for what you attract, or DON'T attract. You are—through your own thoughts and actions—the creator of your own luck. Knowing this, you are in full control of your life.

  7. A WINNER is not afraid to lose.
      A LOSER is secretly afraid of winning.

If you lose a round of golf, what have you actually lost? Chances are you enjoyed a few hours of "fun in the sun" and then returned home, physically and mentally refreshed.

While this is normal, the incredible emphasis that society has placed upon winning, which is taken in an entirely different context than the subject matter of this book, borders on the neurotic. Beating someone at a competitive sport is one thing. Adopting a WINNING ATTITUDE toward life is quite another. The fact is, many fierce competitors gradually develop an almost revengeful attitude toward life. They are no longer just playing a game. Instead, their egos are at stake.

True Winners, on the other hand, know that they will be competing on many levels in life, and that instant victory will not always be theirs. Even so, they do not let their egos get involved. They do not judge their self-worth by how well others are doing.

Winners also know that it is extremely important to be psychologically *prepared* for success. Losers rarely, if ever, are prepared, and in most instances, are even *afraid* of succeeding. Initially, when a Loser wins, he experiences feelings of happiness, enjoyment and euphoria. However, within a short time, these feelings change into feelings of unworthiness, anxiety and mild to severe depression. The way the Loser deals with this is to sabotage his own success so that he can lose again and get back to "where he belongs."

Success brings with it a number of new responsibilities. It can dramatically alter one's life, and also requires that some major changes in thinking and lifestyle take place. In Dostoyevksi's *The Brothers Karamazov*, reference is made to those masses of people who do not crave freedom of self-expression and self-realization so much as they crave freedom from "the fearful burden of free choice." For many, it is actually easier to remain on what they perceive to be a predestined course than to assume responsibility for achieving the life they have always wanted.

How about you? Are you truly committed to living the life of a Winner? If so, it will mean giving up a Loser life-script. Just as you cannot think two thoughts at the same time, you cannot live two life-scripts at the same time.

Are you willing to lose a few rounds before you win? Do you feel you truly *deserve* to win? Do you subconsciously set yourself up to lose because you are secretly afraid of winning? All these questions must be answered before you can become a Winner. Your readiness to accept the role of a Winner will be determined by the life-script you are acting out. Keep in mind that you have the ability to rewrite your script so that it matches your winning desire.

8. WINNERS do it NOW!
LOSERS procrastinate.

Procrastination comes from doing things you think you *have* to do. The truth is, there are only TWO things you have to do. You have to *die* and you have to *live until you die*! Everything else involves a choice.

Winners realize that they are responsible for their choices. No one is making them or forcing them to do what they do. They make their choices and act on them with positive expectation. This requires having a goal and a specific plan for achieving that goal. Most of all, it requires setting priorities for getting things done. If you are presently doing things you should *not* be doing, or avoiding the things you should be doing, then you are a procrastinator. Unfortunately, procrastinators are Losers.

How can you get into the habit of getting things done? The answer lies in the question itself. The operative word is *habit*. The best way to eliminate an unsuccessful habit is to replace it with a successful one, one that works *for* you instead of *against* you.

For the next thirty days, pay close attention to the people you tend to associate with, to the manner in which you spend your time and what you tend to talk about to yourself and others most of the time. How many hours a day do you procrastinate or avoid doing what you need to do to be a Winner? How many hours do you spend in front of the TV, or on the phone, talking to people who do not add to the quality of your life? Is all this talk necessary, or are you just wasting valuable time?

If you eliminated these useless activities, and also did other things to get more hours out of the day, how much difference do you think it would make? Most people would be quick to argue that their schedule is already filled to capacity, that they haven't a second to spare from the moment they get out of bed in the morning until they retire at night. If that is *your* problem, I would like to suggest that you get up one hour earlier each day. By the end of the week, you will have *seven additional hours* to contribute to your success. Over a year's time, that's more than two full weeks!

Start responding to the self-starting command of "I will do it NOW!" Before long you will build a new habit that will become so strong that you will immediately respond and go into action whenever there is *anything* that needs to be done. Remember, Winners are doers! Losers are procrastinators.

9. A WINNER knows that the secret to winning is to *be who you are and become what you were meant to be.*
    A LOSER thinks he can win by "fitting in."

Every human being is as individual and unique as the snow-flakes that fall. What is interesting about this is that what we are willing to accept about snowflakes, we are less inclined to accept about ourselves. Notice how desperately people try to "fit in," how they try to be "normal" in every way.

If you were to ask, no one could tell you the inventor of the standards we tend to measure ourselves by. No one could even tell you how such standards CAME to be standard! Still, we keep trying to "measure up" and prove that we are as typical as the next person. Why? Because we were programmed to get our "strokes" or "payoff" through approval and recognition from parents, teachers, religious leaders, peers and other authority figures.

I am proud to say that in all my life, I have never felt typical, normal or average. My personal quest for self-realization has forced me to recognize my own uniqueness and to give expression to my own special talents, and also, my own idiosyncrasies. Whatever *else* they may be, they are ME!

Throughout my life, well-meaning family and friends tried to dissuade me when I made changes in my lifestyle that conflicted with their expectations. Unfortunately, they attempted to influence my behavior by imposing guilt. I was made to feel guilty for disappointing them or letting them down. This worked until I finally realized that to accept guilt is a choice. Thereafter I chose not to feel guilty.

That your life may be perceived by others as unconventional or unacceptable is not your problem. No matter what you choose to do, most likely somebody is going to feel disappointed. However ideally, in time, others may adjust.

The REAL problem exists in role-playing, in pretending to be something you are not, in living a life-script that was written for you by someone else. The end result is always failure and disappointment. No matter how much you attempt to be something you're not, in the end, you will still consciously or unconsciously seek to become the person you are and were meant to be.

Fortunately, you have a road map to take you from where you are to where you want to be. The path to winning is outlined in the chapters of this book. Follow it and it will lead you back to being yourself and being the person you were meant to be.

10. A WINNER says: "It may be difficult, but it's possible."
   A LOSER says: "It may be possible, but it's too difficult."

To accept that something is difficult but possible, is to act on *positive assumptions*. In this life, where nothing is certain except death, taxes and change, it is necessary to believe that whatever we need to know is always available if we know where to look for the answer. Help is always available, new breakthroughs are just around the corner. History certainly bears this out.

Progress would never have been possible if people were not willing to act upon their positive assumptions. The early pioneers assumed a great deal before they began their long hard journey west. Their primary assumption was that they would *survive*, and that they would actually get where they were going. Fortunately for us, they did.

Whatever you are presently attempting to do, you undoubtedly expect to survive. It is probably not a life-threatening task, and when compared to what the pioneers endured, may seem like nothing at all. Still, you think of it as difficult, perhaps because you have never done it before. In that case, it is time for a few positive assumptions:

1. I will make and keep my commitments.
2. I will find the right people who can help me.
3. I will look for an answer in every problem.
4. I will give up "trying."
5. I will make it okay to be "wrong" and make mistakes.
6. I will create my own "good luck."
7. I will not be afraid to lose before I win.
8. I will do it NOW!

9. I will be who I am and become what I was meant to be.
10. I will accept that all things are possible.

Ignore, at all costs, any negative thinkers who may be inclined to insist that "It can't be done," "It just won't work," "Everyone who has ever attempted it has failed." These same people may also attack your motives, insisting that you are on an "ego trip." Remain committed. Do what needs to be done, even when it is unpopular. Afterward, when these same negative thinkers rally round and say, "I KNEW you could do it!" tell them that you knew it FIRST! You are a Winner because you chose the best bet of all . . . to BET ON YOURSELF!